*"They've found
Forrest Ridley's body
at Apalachee Falls,
up in Watkin County."*

"What the hell do you mean, Forrest Ridley's body?" Edison exclaimed loudly. "The man's a senior partner. He can't be dead!"

And with that, the party froze. Champagne tulips stopped halfway to lips. Words were bitten half-through like cigars. Then the buzz began and grew and grew until it was almost a roar, and in the midst of it, there was a sharper swell of noise as a woman screamed. Samantha glanced about but, strangely, she never did see who had made such an anguished, unladylike sound . . .

BY THE SAME AUTHOR

Impersonal Attractions
Keeping Secrets
Now Let's Talk of Graves*
She Walks in Beauty*
First Kill All the Lawyers*
Then Hang All the Liars*

*Published by POCKET BOOKS

FIRST KILL ALL THE LAWYERS

SARAH SHANKMAN

POCKET BOOKS

New York   London   Toronto   Sydney   Tokyo   Singapore

This book is a work of fiction. Names, characters, places and incidents are either the product of the author's imagination or are used fictitiously. Any resemblance to actual events or locales or persons, living or dead, is entirely coincidental.

An *Original* Publication of POCKET BOOKS

POCKET BOOKS, a division of Simon & Schuster Inc.
1230 Avenue of the Americas, New York, NY 10020

ISBN: 0-671-74893-9

First Pocket Books printing June 1988

10 9 8 7 6 5 4 3 2

POCKET and colophon are registered trademarks of
Simon & Schuster Inc.

Printed in the U.S.A.

FIRST KILL ALL THE LAWYERS was previously published
under the pseudonym of Alice Storey.

To Harvey Klinger

Author's Note

The people listed below have been very helpful to me in the writing of this book, and I would like to thank them.

In Atlanta, for advice and information, Carmen Alonso, J.D., Dr. Kenneth Alonso, Alfred W. Brown and *Brown's Guidebook: Atlanta,* Robert Coram, and Chuck Perry. For continuing encouragement and a home, Cliff Graubart and the Old New York Bookstore.

In Virginia, the Virginia Center for the Creative Arts and its director, William Smart, and staff for residencies which have given me the gift of time.

In New York, Harvey Klinger, my agent, and Jane Chelius, my editor, were wonderful. Every writer should be so lucky as to have two such as these in her corner.

"The first thing we do,
let's kill all the lawyers."

—Shakespeare
   Henry VI, Part II,
   Act IV, Scene ii

FIRST KILL ALL
THE LAWYERS

One

◆

"BILLY GENE CHANDLER WAS MEAN AS A JUNK-yard dog," George said. "Wasn't worth the powder it would've taken to blow him to kingdom come."

Samantha Adams smiled at her uncle across the dining table. She could feel him warming up, and once he got started, he could really tell some stories.

"Why didn't somebody do something about Chandler?" she asked. "Turn him in? Report him?"

George Adams shrugged. "To whom?" And then he waggled his fork at her. "If you don't know the answer to *that* question, you've forgotten more about the South than you've relearned in these few months you've been back."

"You're never going to forgive me for moving to California, are you?" She tilted her face toward the ceiling. "No more than he's going to forgive the engineers for building the interstates through the city, is he, God?"

"God's not going to help you with the big things if

13

you go bothering him with the small fry all the time," volunteered Peaches as she entered the dining room. She peered at Sam's water glass, then into the silver water pitcher. "More water?"

Sam laughed. "Just because I don't drink any- more doesn't mean I want the whole Chattahoochee River poured down my gullet every day, thank you."

"And God doesn't like ugly," Peaches sniffed, then proceeded to clear the salad plates.

"Now, Peaches," Sam protested.

"Don't 'Now, Peaches' me. You heard what I said. He doesn't like ugly."

"I'm sorry. I didn't mean to hurt your feelings. I just meant—"

"I know what you meant." Peaches stood her ground, one hand on a bony hip. "Now, just drink your water and let's change the subject."

It made Peaches cranky when Samantha referred to her alcoholism, to what Peaches called her "being bad to drink." After all, Sam, who had first come to live with them as a young girl, was in part *her* creation. She didn't like anyone, including Sam herself, bad- mouthing her handiwork.

"Tell them to leave you be. Shame on you two, ganging up on her," said Horace as he entered the room carrying a platter of fish.

"That's right." Sam nodded.

"And I guess you've been standing in the kitchen twiddling your thumbs and eavesdropping," Peaches said.

Horace's eyebrows rose a hair, but only a hair, for this routine between the Johnsons, man and wife, was well rehearsed.

"George! Are you going to answer my question or not?" Sam demanded.

"My dear, I'm sorry." He shook his white head in mock seriousness. "In all this commotion, I'd almost forgotten it."

Sam reached across the wide dining room table with a heavy silver serving spoon and rapped her uncle on the knuckles. "Quit playing with me. Now, why didn't any of the good people of Raritan County turn Sheriff Billy Gene Chandler in to the district attorney—or call the governor's office? There must have been *someone* they could have reported him to if he was as awful as you say."

The look bounced from Peaches to Horace to George, then back the other way.

"Don't just roll your eyes at one another. Spill it," said Sam.

"Is that how you earned their praises at the *Chronicle?* Saying things like 'spill it'? That kind of talk may go over big in San Francisco, but you're going to have to develop a more ladylike style if you ever expect to make it in Atlanta," George said.

"I imagine the folks downtown at the *Journal-Constitution* like Samantha's style just fine," said Horace as he boned the fish Peaches had cooked to perfumey perfection. "Otherwise, why would they have stolen her away from that paper in 'Frisco?" He smiled at Sam. "Don't you listen to your Uncle George."

"Will I never be free of the tyranny of my help?" George asked of no one in particular.

And no one answered, for the relationship among George and Peaches and Horace required no response. They had lived together like family in this split-timber Tudor mansion on Fairview Road for almost fifty years.

"Horace, maybe you can answer my question, since George obviously isn't going to," Sam persisted. "He was telling me about Sheriff Billy Gene Chandler from down in Raritan County, and I asked him why nobody reported him for being so corrupt."

"'Cause it wouldn't have done any good." Horace placed fish and vegetables on Samantha and George's plates and placed the plates carefully before them, a style of service he'd adopted to accommodate George's rapidly failing eyesight. "Here's some more wine for you, George," he said, replacing the glass precisely at the one o'clock position. Then he continued, "It's never done any good to complain about lawmen. They just do what they gonna do anyhow."

Samantha shot her uncle a questioning look, then realized he couldn't read it from that far away—but she was wrong. As his vision dimmed, George Adams was honing his already sharp intuition.

"No, Sam, Horace doesn't mean just blacks. White folks would gain nothing either by complaining."

Race had always been so negligible an issue in this household that the mention of it was not an impoliteness, as it would have been in many quarters.

"That's right," Horace continued. "Puff adders like that Sheriff Chandler, they'd just as soon poison their own kind. Fact, what I heard about him with women, he didn't discriminate when it came to color."

"Now, don't go talking about that, 'specially at the dinner table," Peaches warned, all the while busying herself brushing at imaginary crumbs so she wouldn't miss a word.

"What *about* women?" Samantha's curiosity sat up.

"Sheriff Chandler was known for a peculiar way of gaining the attentions of those whom he fancied," George explained. "When he took a shine to a lady, if she didn't return his interest, he just locked her up."

"He *what?*"

"Yep. Then sent his deputy out for a moonpie and a *long* RC Cola while he had his way with her."

"And those people put up with that?"

"Those people are afraid, Sam. They're terrified of men like Billy Gene Chandler—and with good reason. That's what I've been trying to tell you ever since you got me off on this subject. Rural sheriffs in this state rule their counties like fiefdoms. Once in office, they're there for life. You cross the man, and you're either going to have to pay the price, settle with him somehow, or move out—fast. There's a lot of ignorance and in-growth in these little backwater places. They take care of things in their own way."

"I can't believe I grew up not knowing this. What was I thinking about when I was a girl?" But she *had* known some of it, if only subliminally.

"Boys," Peaches answered. "Pajama parties. Nail polish. Normal things."

Sam ignored her. "What do you mean, 'take care of things in their own way'? Like how?"

"You name it—murder, rape, robbery. They keep it all very close to home," George said.

"By that you mean it never makes the papers."

The other three exchanged looks.

"Makes the papers! Why, Sam, it never gets to trial. Most of the time charges aren't even pressed. Rural justice is much more primitive than that." George sipped his wine. "A man kills someone, let's say. Now, unless the one who was killed *deserved* killing in the sheriff's eyes, then within a year that murderer is going to find himself dead too, unless he has the good sense to move out."

"George, you are making this up," Sam protested. "Why, all this reeks of the *Old* South. This is the *New* South, darlin'. Don't try to tell me nothing's changed while I've been away. I can see changes everywhere I turn."

And that, in part, was true. But deep down, Sam knew that many things about the South had not changed and never would, and that was in part why she had returned to it. One of the things she'd always said, as a stranger in the even stranger land of California, was that she'd never regretted growing up Southern. Most certainly the South had its dark side, and she was among the first to point out its obvious flaws. But it had its charms, too, its gentility, its beauty, and, not least, its humor—none of which she had ever seen the likes of in all her travels. And although the K Marts and the tract houses and the McDonald's in some ways made it look like other places, it wasn't.

"Unfortunately, some things that ought to change don't," George answered her charge.

"So you're going to sit here and tell me that most of the justice in this state is still dealt out catch-as-catch-can by a handful of fat rednecks?"

"Well, I don't imagine they're all fat, and as you'll remember we mostly call them crackers, but yes, that's what I'm saying."

"And no one does a thing about it?" Sam demanded.

"Well, only every once in a while. And usually only when it can't be helped. I mean, the mess Sheriff

Chandler got himself in had nothing whatsoever to do with local folks—that was on account of the Drug Enforcement Administration."

"Because he was . . ."

"Because he was helping some boys fly such bodacious amounts of cocaine into his county that the hillsides were beginning to look like winter in Vermont."

"And you think corruption like this goes on throughout the state?"

"No, I don't think so. I know so," George said. "My esteemed fellow partners at Simmons and Lee didn't give me that gold watch when I retired for being stupid."

"So you agree with me there's a story there?"

"Of course there's a story. But what I am trying to impress on you in my humble, inarticulate way is that you would most likely get yourself killed investigating it."

Sam ignored that little bit of business since they both knew that George Adams was one of the most gifted orators ever to address a Georgia courtroom.

"Now you should listen to him," said Horace, reaching in to remove Samantha's empty plate.

"Horace, maybe you could just hold up cue cards for Sam."

Horace went on as if George hadn't spoken. "You don't want to be messing around with country lawmen. That is *bad* business."

"I don't know why she wants to be poking around in such troublesome things anyway," Peaches put in. "Why can't you write about nice things?"

"I did that story about your reading program," Sam reminded her.

Peaches sniffed. "I hope you didn't do it just because you thought it would shut me up."

"No, I did it because it's something worthwhile that people ought to know about. But you know that was way out of my territory. One doesn't *investigate* things that are nice."

"Well, you ought to."

"Next thing you know, Peaches, you're going to tell me that my place is in the home."

That was a joke of long standing, for the Adams home, which Peaches ruled as housekeeper, was frequently the last place one would find her. Having returned to school and graduated from college in her early forties, Peaches had never looked back once she got going and was now, among other things, one of the mainstays of the city's Each One Teach One campaign against illiteracy.

And Sam knew that Peaches was as proud of Sam's professional accomplishments as if she were her own daughter, but it was Peaches' way to grumble. It was the Adams way to tease, so Sam kept going. "Or you're going to try to get me married off again. Sure you don't want me to find myself a nice doctor or lawyer and settle down?"

"That's okay. You just go right ahead and make fun of an old woman," Peaches said.

Horace played an imaginary violin behind Peaches' back.

"I see you there, Horace Johnson!" She swatted at him without turning around.

"Didn't I tell you?" Horace asked. "Witches have eyes in the back of their heads."

"Go right on ahead. But one of these days she's going to wake up dead and be sorry she didn't do something normal." Peaches turned and pushed through the swinging door. "Doctor, lawyer, indeed," she grumbled as she went. *"That* wouldn't kill her, at least."

"Why don't you say what's on your mind, Peaches?" Sam called after her.

"Speaking of lawyers," George said, shoving back from the table, "if I could interrupt you, there's something I want to talk about, Sam. Horace"—he nodded at the other man—"thanks for the lovely dinner. Now, if you'll excuse us, we're going to move into the library where we can hear ourselves think."

The room was warm and comfortable, its walls lined with cherrywood bookshelves that Horace, whose hobby was woodworking, had built years ago. There wasn't room for another volume here; the shelves were jammed with George's collection of first-edition fiction and a vast assortment of oversized travel volumes. His law books were in his study; more bookcases lined hallways and bedroom walls throughout the large three-story house.

Horace had laid a fire in the glass-screened fireplace, for even though it was early April and the air was heavy with the scent of Atlanta's famous azaleas, dogwood, and wisteria, this particular evening there was a bit of a nip in the air. And Horace, who like George was almost seventy, knew all too well that the older folks got, the colder their bones.

Samantha sat in one of a pair of brown leather easy chairs and gazed with affection at her uncle, who sat in the other. He had always been her favorite relative, and she his. When her parents had died in the 1962 plane crash near Paris that killed 122 members of the

Atlanta Art Association, other aunts and uncles and family friends had offered to take her in, but it was George who had prevailed.

"I need her as much as she needs me," he'd said, and the others had acquiesced. These two had always had a special bond. In fact, it had been George rather than Samantha's father who had chosen her name—at the time hardly a popular appellation for a little Southern belle.

"Sam Adams is a venerable choice," George had said at her christening. And it was also a legitimate family name, the Atlanta Adamses tracing their ancestry back to that Boston clan, which made Sam a member of the DAR as well as a Daughter of the Confederacy. "Besides, I looked up *Samantha,* and the name means *listener,*" her uncle had said. "God knows we could use somebody in this family who can do that."

So it was natural that George and Peaches and Horace had adopted the favored but orphaned Samantha. They had held her hand through her grief and delighted as she reclaimed a personality filled with light and joy. Sometimes, said George, too much joy; when Sam reached the full riotousness of adolescence, he'd remodeled the second floor of the house and banished her, her dogs, her telephone, her rock and roll, and her wild band of giggling girlfriends upstairs.

George had taken her everywhere with him, including to Europe twice before she was fifteen. He wanted her horizons to have no limits. When it was time for college, she'd sent off for all the catalogs, and she and George had visited schools on both coasts. Then, having taken a good look, she'd decided, much to George's delight, to stay home. Atlanta's Emory University had been good enough for her uncle; it was good enough for her. She made dean's list her freshman year—and then that following summer, she met Beau. Only six months later, she'd fled to California and Stanford, taking George's heart with her. That had been almost twenty years ago.

"Horace has brought you a small pot of coffee. Shall I serve you some?" George asked.

At her nod, he poured her a cup of Horace's bracing brew and himself a tot of cognac. All his moves were careful, practiced. He'd been taking lessons from the Lighthouse for the Blind in "the avoidance of making a total ass of oneself," as he called it.

He was philosophical about his predicament: if he had to go blind, he said, at least the cause was something more exotic than simple old age. He had contracted river blindness while tromping around the Amazonian wilderness of Brazil. Yet he wouldn't have given up a moment of his world-trekking, even if the eventual price could have been predicted.

"I received an interesting telephone call today," he said after toasting her health. "From Liza Ridley, the daughter of Forrest Ridley."

"One of your old partners."

"Yes, I thought you might remember him."

"Not very clearly. But I remember your talking about his work," Sam said.

"Always solid and sometimes brilliant. Anyway, I've known young Liza since she was a twinkle in Forrest's eye, and I'm very fond of her. Bright girl. Different. Gives her mother fits, I'm sure."

"Sounds like a young lady after my own heart."

"I suspected you'd think so. That's why I thought I'd ask you to do me this favor."

Sam cocked a finger at him. "Pow!" she said. She should have known George was up to something.

He smiled and continued, "Liza said she didn't know who else to talk to about this. She thinks her father is missing or in some kind of trouble. Seems he calls her every Saturday morning over at Agnes Scott College, where she's a senior, and they make their bets with one another on the weekend ball games. This is the second Saturday in a row he's missed."

"Why doesn't she just call him at home?" Sam suggested.

"He's not *at* home. She said her mother, Queen—I don't know if you ever met her—Queen told her he's away on business."

"Queen?"

"Queen."

"Of the Bitsie, Bootsie, Muffy, Muggsie school?" Even though she'd grown up with them, Sam had always found these WASP nicknames ridiculous.

"The same genre."

"So why doesn't *Queen*'s word take care of it?"

"Ridley's never failed to call her before, even when he was out of the country. It seems this betting business is something they've done together since Liza was a little girl."

"Only child?"

"Yes. And the apple of Forrest's eye. Even though Liza, as I said, is a most unexpected product of the Ridley environment, a bit of a bohemian. He dotes on her."

"Why doesn't she get her father's number from her mother and just call him?" Sam asked.

"Liza said Queen was rather vague about exactly where he is. San Francisco, she said, but wasn't forthcoming with a phone number."

"Sounds like a family matter to me, George. And more than a little silly. I know you've always loved doing these bits of skulking around when the Four Hundred wanted their dirty linen kept private, but this doesn't seem worth your trouble. Forrest Ridley will probably call tomorrow, and it'll all be over."

"Maybe." George was thoughtful. "Maybe not."

Sam leaned forward and played with her coffee spoon, keeping her hands busy the way reformed smokers do when they'd rather be puffing on a cigarette. "Do you suspect something?"

"I don't know. Ridley's such a straight shooter, such a dependable man. I find this a bit odd."

"Your antennae working overtime?"

"Maybe. In any case, I've arranged for you to visit with Queen Ridley tomorrow."

"What? Me?" Sam sat up straight. "George! I don't have time for this. Have you forgotten I have a job?"

"Were you going in to the office tomorrow?" A five-year-old child couldn't have asked the question with less guile.

"Yes, as a matter of fact, I *was*. I'm going to talk to Hoke about this sheriff business. And just because I work my own hours, George, does not mean that you should make appointments for me!"

"My dear, I'm very sorry."

With that, George rubbed his eyes with a weary gesture. Then he looked up at her with a face so contrite that she was suddenly embarrassed at her flare of temper. This was George, her beloved George. How could she deny him such a small favor?

"Oh, no, *I'm* sorry." She reached over and patted his hand. "I didn't mean to be so sharp. Of course I'll do it for you."

"Good." He grinned, his expression just the tiniest bit triumphant.

And Samantha realized that she had been bamboozled by one of the wiliest of that most conniving, finagling breed of cat, the Southern lawyer.

"Damn you!"

"Ah, ah, ah." He waggled a finger at her. "Too late. A promise is a promise."

An hour later Sam sat in her bedroom before her dressing table mirror, toweling dry her dark curls. She leaned over and peered at her face, pulling with a forefinger at the corner of one eye. "Still holding, old girl," she said aloud to her reflection. She chalked up her preservation to good genes, lots of sleep, eight glasses of water a day, and miles of fast walking.

The spacious yellow and white rectangular room, formerly the sun porch, was her favorite in this second-floor apartment—her old digs, which were still being refurbished. Peaches and Horace were above on the third floor, next to the attic studio George had let out for a long time to an artist friend. Sam liked the feeling of being in the middle, once again smack in the bosom of her family.

"I made the right decision in coming back, Harpo," she said to the small white Shih Tzu who was lying belly-up on the carpet. He was giving her the look that meant she'd take him for a late-night walk if she were really a good person.

She picked him up and gave him a nuzzle. "In a little while. Hold on."

Then she glanced from the small dog to the silver-framed photograph of Sean O'Reilly that sat on her dressing table. It was Sean who had given her Harpo when the puppy was only a fluff-ball.

It had been the death of Sean, the chief of detectives in San Francisco and her lover, that had caused her to return to Atlanta. Yes, there'd been the fortuitous invitation at about the same time from the *Constitution,* too; the paper had made the deal very sweet. But she would have flown to the consoling arms of George even without the offer.

What irony—that she, who had almost killed herself with booze during her twenties but had been sober for almost ten years, should lose the man she loved to a drunk driver. The tragedy had felt like a replay of her parents' deaths. Afraid she was going crazy, afraid of being tempted by the bottle, she'd known it was time to go home again. Nowhere else in the world offered such comfort.

Harpo picked up his rubber carrot, dropped it on her foot, and growled. Playtime was the only time he ever spoke.

"Here, silly." She threw the toy to the other end of the long room. The dog chased it, then sat down beside it and stared at her.

"Fetch."

He didn't budge.

"Rotten. Spoiled rotten."

She walked to the other end of the room, picked up

the little dog, then turned and gazed out the window across the street toward the Talbot house. She stayed there, her attention focused.

Lights were on downstairs, in the living room, dining room, and kitchen. Miriam Talbot was probably finishing up her dinner dishes. Sam's eye traveled up the red brick to the second floor. All was dark there, including the front room on the left, which she'd spent her entire nineteenth summer watching, the bedroom that had belonged to Miriam Talbot's son, Beau.

"Son-of-a-bitch!"

The words startled her, as if someone else had spoken. Harpo squirmed and stared up at her.

"Not you," she told him, laughing, and put him down on the floor.

But she kept standing there. She threw open the multi-paned casement window and took a deep breath of the evening air. She closed her eyes and thought she could almost smell Miriam's roses. Beau had once blanketed her with those roses. At that thought, an ancient pain twisted in her gut.

It was amazing. Almost twenty years had passed since Beau had broken her young girl's heart and caused her to flee Atlanta. All that water under the bridge. She smiled wryly. All that branch water and all that bourbon. All the faces. All the other bodies she'd awakened to. All the roller-coaster ups and downs and all the long, flat, dry spaces. And still she could stand at this window and look across the street to where she'd met Dr. Beau Talbot, the too-handsome intern home for the summer before he began his New York residency, and feel exactly the same emotions. The excitement. The rush. The exhilaration. And the thrumming, drumming pain.

She clutched the window sash. Jesus! Was it always going to be the same? When she was eighty and wrinkled into some apple-doll caricature of her younger self, would all her emotions remain in place? Not just about Beau, but the same jealousies, loves, hates, the same messy mishmash of emotions one felt about oneself and other members of the human race? Well, why not? She couldn't remember it ever being any different since she remembered feeling at all; the basic sense of self, the voice inside her head, had always been the same.

Now that voice found words once more, and she threw them out into the April night.

"You son-of-a-bitch!" she yelled, slammed the window shut for punctuation, and stood there grinning. Well, now, *that* felt better.

She hadn't yelled all those years ago. She'd pulled her blanket over her head and moaned. It had taken George and Peaches days to get the story out of her. Beau had changed his mind. No, he didn't want her to follow him to New York, to transfer to NYU. He didn't want her at all. There was another girl. Someone he'd met before, in Boston. He didn't know how it had happened; he hadn't meant for it to. They were getting married right away. He was sorry.

Two weeks later and ten pounds lighter, she had climbed out of her bed and begun to pack. Her destination wasn't New York, but rather the opposite coast.

"It's too late to get into Stanford," George had protested.

Sam had given him a look that said she knew he could help her do anything he wanted. And he could. He'd made the calls and pulled the strings even as he'd argued, insisting there was no reason for her to leave.

But there was. Everywhere she turned, Samantha had run into Beau's ghost. Every place they had ever been during that long, delicious summer was perfumed with their scent and echoed with the sound of their leftover laughter. No, she couldn't stay in Atlanta.

"I have to, I must," she'd said again and again, even as she and George and Peaches piled into that year's Lincoln and Horace drove them to the airport. All the way to San Francisco she'd hummed under her breath Janis Joplin's paean to pain, "A Little Piece of My Heart." Janis had known what she was talking about.

Now Samantha was back.

She'd come home.

It wasn't the first time, of course. She'd dropped in for occasional brief visits during her California sojourn—just long enough to say hello and good-bye and register the changes.

Atlanta. It *had* changed. And yet . . . *Plus ça change, plus c'est la même chose.* She was only now beginning to discover the static places and the fluid. Whole neighborhoods had disappeared to satisfy the appetite of the freeway monster. There were more Yankee voices. And there were newcomers on the North Side who had never even *been* downtown. But the Varsity still made chili dogs. Manners still counted. And the television preachers still had an audience, as did the fulminating racists—in a town that was now sixty percent black and well into its second black mayor. Ah, Atlanta. Was *she* too Yankee for it now? Could their respective changes find a common ground? Discovering the answers to those questions was going to be interesting.

During those years away when people asked her, as they were wont to do, "Why did you leave the South?" she'd answered flippantly, as was *her* wont, "Because of a summer romance. Because of a broken heart." She'd said that for years and years and years, long past the time, perhaps, when she should have forgotten.

But this was not a thing that Sam would forget or ever take lightly. She'd come to live in this house when her parents had died. It was Beau's desertion that had banished her. Now Sean was gone, and she had returned. She stared out at the house where Beau had once lived and heard the old music come back. She softly whistled the refrain to Joplin's "Ball and Chain."

Of course, Beau wasn't the only reason she'd stayed away for so long. Things began, and then they kept rolling. At Stanford, on the rebound, she'd found and married, then later divorced, her bearded draft resister. She'd floated along on that river of bourbon and branch water. Year followed year and things got better and things got worse and then better again, and she'd become Sam Adams, Renowned Girl Reporter. She'd found success and she'd found Sean, and then, hell— it was a life. Which she *certainly* hadn't lived in California just to avoid Beau Talbot. Why, she hadn't known for ages that he had moved back home—and become the state's chief medical examiner.

She turned from the window and plopped herself once again before her dressing table mirror.

She was going to run into him. It was only a matter

of time. An investigative reporter could no more avoid a medical examiner than pigs could fly—not unless, of course, she gave up on murder. But murder was her specialty.

Sam's series on a serial killer in San Francisco had won her journalistic prizes, had earned her the reputation that had gotten her this cushy spot on the *Constitution*, naming her own stories, answering only to the managing editor.

Yet she'd heard herself telling George recently that she was thinking about pursuing other avenues, leaving the blood and gore to some other reporter. She'd had her bellyful of middle-of-the-night morgue visits, of psychopaths, of interviewing families who were neck-deep in grief.

George had nodded when she told him all this. And she knew that he knew that she was lying through her teeth.

Two

◆

T HE FIRST TIME SAMANTHA HAD STEPPED INTO MANAG-
ing editor Hoke Toliver's office, he'd stubbed out
one of the hundred cigarettes he would smoke that
day and said, "Dammit, there are so frigging many
reasons I can't sleep with you."

It was an interesting beginning, Sam thought, not
that she hadn't heard some doozies in her time.

"Shoot," she'd said. "I'll admit I'm curious."

"How old are you?"

"In the thirty-five-to-forty ozone. None of your
business."

"See, I *knew* you were younger than Lois."

"Lois?"

"My wife."

"Lois doesn't like you sleeping with younger
women?"

"Nope. Makes her crankier than a prom queen with
a fresh zit on her nose."

"Well, that's one," Sam had remarked.

"Two, I saw you across the room at a meeting last

week, and I promised myself I'd never sleep with anybody in the program."

"Which one?"

"Which one what?"

"Which A.A. meeting?"

"The one at St. Philip's."

"I didn't see you."

"I know." He'd pulled his mouth down at the corners, run one hand through the first crew cut she'd seen since the late fifties, and with the other hauled up his sagging pants. "I was sitting over in smoking, hiding my stupefyingly good looks under a bushel, 'cause I didn't want you to get distracted from the qualifying speaker."

"Fat chance," she'd said.

Not that he wasn't good-looking; he was, in a crew-cut, hound-doggish sort of way. But at that particular meeting, the woman who had been talking about her experiences with alcohol could have stood off Joan Rivers in mouth-to-mouth combat.

"So if you don't find fresh meat at meetings, and I assume you don't hang out in bars anymore, where do you find the lucky darlings?"

He'd tweaked his own jowls, which flapped in the lingering blue haze in his office, lit another cigarette, and answered, "At my health club."

Samantha had to laugh.

"The third reason is that you're smarter than I am. Or that's what the new boss-man, the one we imported all the way from *New* York, says."

"Does, does he?"

"Yep. Says you're the smartest thing he's ever seen in a skirt."

"Or out—" She'd caught herself, but Hoke was far

34

too fast. He was already grinning as he said, "Yep, out of one, too. And I imagine Mr. Boss's seen some real smart skirtless women up there in *New* York."

Samantha knew better than to rise to that kind of bait, particularly since she knew that Hoke was, in more ways than one, blowing smoke. But she hadn't been able to resist.

"Did it ever occur to you that there's a fourth reason we might not sleep together?"

"Yep, I did think that like every other smart woman, you might occasionally have an extraordinary moment of the dumbs when you might choose to pass up such a stud hoss as myself, but I figured it'd pass. You'd get over it."

Sam was standing in his office now. "Hoke, I want to do a series on the corruption of rural sheriffs."

"'Scuse me," he said, hitting himself on one ear. "I thought you said you wanted to commit suicide. I must have misunderstood you, right?"

Samantha flopped down in the reasonable facsimile of a wooden chair that sat before his battered desk. "Why is everybody so skittish on this subject?"

"Like who?"

"Like my Uncle George."

"I've always respected George Adams's judgment. One of the finest barristers the South has ever known. Question is, why're you here seeking a second opinion?" He lit one cigarette off another. "Now, why don't you mosey on over to Macon and do something with that mother-raper's been working the fancy neighborhoods? Be a lot safer. And get you the front page."

"Hoke, did you know that Billy Gene Chandler

35

from Raritan County used to lock up women so he could have sex with them?"

"You want to trade stories, woman?" Hoke leaned back in his chair and exhaled a plume of smoke. "Well, you've come to the right place. I'll tell you one: Sheriff Nelson over in Cleveland County *personally* killed a white Yankee reporter lady who came around asking questions about the Klan."

"I don't believe that."

"It doesn't matter what you believe. He did it. 'Course, he made it look like an accident. He's also murdered a couple of traveling salesmen and I don't know how many nameless vagrants."

"Why?"

"Why?" Hoke shook his head. "'Cause he has a taste for it. He *likes* it. It makes him feel good. Plus, in the case of the reporter, Nelson rides with the Klan himself sometimes and didn't want her jerking on *his* bedsheets. Now, if you want more, there are the badge-toting boys who still sell moonshine up in north Georgia, though not so many of 'em these days 'cause there's lots more money in drugs. I guess they got to supplement that twenty-five thou they're dragging down somehow. And simple graft just ain't as profitable as it used to be."

"What else?"

"What else you want? Want to hear about the gambling, the cockfights, the dog racing, the prostitution, the little girls they auction off to the richest dirty old man? You just imagine any old pot full of shit you can think of, and you're going to find a sheriff with his finger in it."

"So why doesn't somebody do something about it?" Sam demanded.

"Sister-baby, that's what I love about you California liberals."

"I was born in this very city, Hoke. In Emory Hospital."

"Thanks for reminding me. Reckon I'll call 'em up when you leave and see on exactly *which* date. 'Thirty-five to forty,'" he muttered under his breath. "Give me a frigging break."

She'd fed him that line months ago, and he was chewing on it still. But that was okay. That was why he was a good editor. He never forgot a single thing, never missed a trick. "You didn't answer my question. Why doesn't somebody do something about these bastards?"

"You think all you have to do is get a bunch of folks together and smoke some dope and march around holding your fingers in a V chanting 'Love and peace,' and everything is going to change. Your question is stupid."

"I *don't* think it's still the sixties," she said calmly, ignoring the insult. She'd been called names by better men than Hoke, and she knew they resorted to the tactic because she made them nervous. For just about the time their eyes fell to her breasts or her legs and their fantasies began, which made them antsy enough, she'd start with her never-ending questions, which made some of them visibly twitch.

"No, maybe you don't," Hoke said. "But even after you've seen all those corpses, all those *pieces* of corpses"—Sam could tell she'd really pushed his buttons now—"and mushy things that *used* to be corpses, after all the violence you've witnessed *supposed* human beings wreak on one another, you can stand there like you're wearing white gloves on your way to a DAR tea, and ask me *why?* You still think you can change basically rotten, no-good sons-of-bitches?"

"No," said Sam, smiling. "But I think we can catch 'em."

That cut off his water for a minute. But only for a minute.

"They're gonna love it when you bust your pretty ass." He hooked a thumb toward his office door.

Samantha knew he was speaking the truth. Her privileges had stirred up resentment among the other reporters who had to work within the system, answering to the assistant city editor, coming into the office every day, taking assignments rather than playing it by ear and sniffing out their own stories, then following them to ground. If she were on their side of the fence, she'd hate her guts, too.

"They're just waiting for you to belly-up," Hoke said.

"I know that. They want it bad enough to break out the champagne if I get myself shot?"

"Might." He nodded. "Just might." And then he dropped the banter. "If you insist on going further with this, *Miz* Adams, you do your research in the morgue"—he pointed a finger in the direction of the paper's files—"and the library." Then he aimed his cigarette at her. "And before you do any nosing around, we'll talk."

Samantha smiled.

"You hear me?" he said.

She was already halfway out the door. "I hear you." She paused. "Now, remember, darlin', don't drink, and go to meetings. But not with lust in your heart."

She'd heard the two words he flung back at her before.

Sam stood on the sidewalk in front of the newspaper's building on Marietta Street. In San Francisco, the *Chronicle's* offices were right downtown also, close to the old heart of the city. Two blocks along Marietta was Five Points, where all the power—business, banking, government—and traffic converged. George's offices, until his retirement a few years ago, had been in a new, tall, cold white tower at that hub. It wasn't San Francisco's Union Square, but then, what was?

To Sam's eye, downtown Atlanta, despite some recent construction including the highly touted but architecturally misbegotten Portman complex, was frumpy. And despite the best efforts of the police and the chamber of commerce, it was still dangerous after dark. It didn't have San Francisco's sea breezes, sophistication, foghorns, or Victorian charm. But, especially on a clear spring morning like this one, Atlanta had a lot going for it. The air was absolutely heady with the smell of spring flowers, which made bright splashes of color everywhere. Despite the surface slowness, there was a sense of hustle here, not the fist in the face that was New York, but an energy that hadn't been seen in San Francisco since the Gold Rush. This New Atlanta was a city on the move. And its magnolia-mellowed moxie made Sam happy, because it generated news.

She wheeled her silvery blue BMW out of a parking garage and headed north on Peachtree Street toward Queen Ridley's house.

How did she let George get her into these things?

What she really wanted was to drop by her gym for an exercise class or maybe a swim. What she *didn't* want was an Atlanta ladies' lunch, an over-mayonnaised chicken salad on iceberg lettuce and a glass of pre-sweetened iced tea. She bet herself five bucks that's what Queen's menu would be. Nor was she particularly looking forward to meeting the lady. Another Atlanta powermonger's wife was hardly going to be a novelty.

Well, at least the drive was pleasant. Sam loved Peachtree Street, the parade of old hotels and churches, the onion domes and minarets of the Fox Theater mixed in with the towers of Coca-Cola, Life of Georgia, Southern Bell. She never drove down the street that she didn't think of Margaret Mitchell, who had lived all her life on or near it and who had been killed by a taxicab while crossing Peachtree at Fourteenth. It was at that very intersection that Colony Square now stood—a tall, handsome complex of hotel space, residences, and offices, mostly for advertising agencies, a proud standard-bearer of Atlanta on the move. Mitchell's girlhood home, three blocks farther north, had been replaced by an office building, too. What would Scarlett have thought of all this? It was Sam's considered opinion that that hot-tempered scrapper, who had never been shy about going after what she wanted, in this day and age would probably be the president of one of those Colony Square ad agencies, delivering the competition their balls on power breakfast plates.

Scarlett sure as hell wouldn't be sitting at home in one of the mansions that made up the winding neighborhood of Ansley Park just behind Colony Square—not like Queen Ridley. Scarlett wouldn't have been a typical debutante, brought up to smile, acquiesce, marry well, and then hold on tooth and nail for the rest of her life to the money and power of the man she'd snagged. No, Ms. O'Hara would be out there on her own mixing it up—well, as much as the good old boys would let her. For Scarlett would have learned—the hard way probably, as Sam was learning day by day—that no matter how strong, how competent the woman, in Atlanta men still called the shots.

The Ridleys' wide-porched white mansion was set well back from the winding street. Lona, the housekeeper who answered the chiming doorbell, was a tall, long-necked black woman who carried herself as if her willowy neck were ringed with silver bangles. Sam found herself straightening her shoulders as she followed the regal woman into the living room.

Queen Ridley rose to greet Samantha from one of three identical white silk sofas in the all-white room. A short, sleek blond woman, she looked as if she'd been enameled. She was exactly what Sam had expected, the quintessence of her name and station at the top of Atlanta society. She was all of a piece, Queen. Every single surface was absolute shining perfection—her nails, her hair, her trousers and shirt of taupe polished cotton, the sculpted ivory and gold jewelry at her ears and wrists. Her engagement ring was a ten-carat marquise canary diamond. Her careful but heavy makeup was flawless. Mid-thirties was what she looked, but Sam thought she was probably on the shady side of forty-five.

"I am *so* glad to see you," Queen gushed in that honeyed, *r*-dropping accent that belongs to ladies of substance in the Deep South. The intonation is also heard in women's voices in Southampton, in Newport, and on Park Avenue, for it is money that makes that sound. "I said to Forrest that I was going to beat him with a stick if he didn't have you and George over to dinner soon. It's just scandalous that you've been back in town this long and we haven't had a party for you."

Samantha knew that all this palaver, all this assumed coziness, was Queen's way of saying that George had been rude in not having *them* over to take a look at the prodigal niece who'd come back home.

"Why, that's so kind of you," Sam murmured. She was rapidly remembering how to play these particular games, how to say without a note of irony, "Isn't that sweet?" "Isn't that interesting?" and "I'm *so* sorry I missed you." It was like shooting. Once you'd developed the skill to hit bull's-eyes, you never forgot. "George has, of course, had wonderful things to say about you both. I'm afraid I don't remember . . . did you know my parents?"

"Why, no, *I* didn't, though I think my mother was in school with yours."

Sam nodded and murmured, "Of course." Then she let it go. No percentage in pushing the point.

But obviously Queen didn't think so. "*Forrest* knew your mother, of course. He's a good bit older than I."

Of course. There was no use looking that much younger than your age if you couldn't push it.

"So how are you liking it back in Atlanta? I'm sure you must find us all a bit provincial."

"Not at all."

"Well, you know how it is. Most people get away, why, they never come back." Queen sniffed and brushed at the hard, shiny surface of her slacks.

"Though I never could understand why anybody would want to leave in the first place, go off somewhere with a bunch of strangers—you don't even know who their people are."

No, you don't, Sam thought. And you don't worry about it, either. You don't worry about how long their family's belonged to the Driving Club, or how long they've had their money, or whether or not the silver they're pouring your coffee from has the distinction of having been buried in the garden to keep it out of the hands of the bloody Yankees. You don't worry about any of that at all.

"Well, some of those strangers can be pretty interesting," she said.

"I'm sure." Queen smiled politely, then called to Lona as if to save Sam the embarrassment of elaborating on that remark.

Who were those strangers of whom Queen was so contemptuous? Blacks. That was number one on her list for sure. Communists. Atheists. Dykes. *Thanks for the drink, Queen. Say, have you ever screwed a colored communist atheist dyke?*

"I'll have a glass of water, or soda, or iced tea, whatever's convenient," Sam said to Lona, who inclined her long neck in answer. The clank of the imaginary silver bangles was distinct.

"Yes'm," she said, but the *m* was very soft.

"Well," Queen laughed with raised eyebrows, *"I'm* not afraid of a little tiddly before noon. Make that a vodka and tonic for me, Lona."

The black woman dipped her head and disappeared from the room.

"George hasn't brought you to *anything* at the Driving Club, or at least we haven't seen you. Of

43

course, we haven't seen George there in ages either. What *have* you two been doing?"

Samantha had once, when she was very young, accompanied Uncle George to the Piedmont Driving Club—that bastion of conservatism, wealth, power, dry-cheeked social kisses, and tuna sandwiches on white bread—perched on the edge of Piedmont Park. And even then, once was enough. When George had offered her the chance to make her debut there, she'd said, "I'll pass." He'd laughed and instead bought her the Triumph sports car in British racing green she'd been lusting after.

"Well, you know Uncle George doesn't go out as much as he used to, with his vision," Sam began.

"Oh, yes, poor thing, but you know, dear, you shouldn't let that keep you in. A beautiful woman like you, new blood in Atlanta, why, we could have you matched up with someone at the club in no time."

"Yes, but I do have a career, and—"

Queen waved a hand in dismissal and charged on. "I just don't know what's gotten into the heads of women these days, pretending they don't need men. Why, what I wish for every woman in the world is that she could be as happy as Forrest and I have been. Now, that may sound a bit like I'm tooting my own horn, but I mean it. You just don't know what bliss is until you've been married to a man like Forrest."

"I'm sure . . ."

"Well, of course, not that I'm going to let you have *him.*" Queen's laughter was well oiled, rehearsed, mechanical. She was as cool, Sam thought, as the drink Lona had just handed her. "It was love at first sight for me and Forrest twenty-five years ago. I shouldn't say that." She dimpled. "It gives my age away."

Only a woman who looked as good as Queen, Sam thought, could deliver that line so silkily.

"We ought to get your membership in the Junior League transferred, too. There are so many girls who have heard about you and are dying to meet you."

"I'm afraid I've never belonged." Neither had Sam picked up her membership in the other societies to which her accident of birth entitled her—though she had arrived at Stanford in time to join the SDS. For a few years there, she'd joined anything that would give her license to smoke dope and drink Southern Comfort, yell at the police and throw smoke bombs.

"Well, my goodness! I find that hard to believe, Samantha. But never mind." Queen reached over and patted her on the knee. "We can take care of that."

Sam started to protest, but then she reminded herself that she needn't worry. It was all politesse. The moment she was gone, Queen would forget all about her.

"Now, where shall we have our lunch? In the little dining room or in the sun room? Or we could eat out on the back veranda. Come." Queen stood.

How could the woman sit in polished cotton without creating creases? But then, Queen was not a woman to brook *any* kind of wrinkles.

"I'll show you the house."

This was an old Atlanta tradition, the obligatory house tours that went up and down, on forever through room after room of impeccable decorator decor, floors you could eat from. Queen Ridley's palace was no exception.

Her decorator had carried the all-white theme everywhere. There was white in every luxurious fabric imaginable, and even the old wide-planked floors had been bleached to bone. Glints of brass and the dark cherry of English antiques provided contrast to the acres of powdery white.

They passed Lona in the kitchen arranging a salad of fancy greens—endive, watercress, arugula—and goat cheese. Not a bite of chicken in sight. Nouvelle cuisine had hit the Old South. Sam was relieved to be wrong for a change.

"You can serve us out back," said Queen.

Again, that elided "Yes'm."

Settled into wicker chairs at a table covered in white-on-white checks, they sipped fresh drinks, and Samantha complimented Queen on her beautiful yard. Azaleas abounded.

"Forrest spoils me so," Queen was saying. "In addition to Lona full-time, I have a gardener in every day and a houseman three times a week. I don't know what I'd do without them."

What do you do *with* them? Sam wondered. But she knew the answer to that—the same things beautifully useless women had always done to fill their days: endless rounds of hair appointments and fittings and luncheons, teas and parties, club and tennis dates, all of which didn't amount to a hill of beans.

"I do wish I could meet Forrest. He's not home, is he?"

"Ah-ha!" Queen laughed. "I'd almost forgotten, dear, that George said Liza had called him about her 'missing-in-action' father." Sam could hear the implied quotes. "She is the *most* headstrong girl sometimes. I must apologize for her. But"—and she gave

Sam a dazzling smile—"if she hadn't called George, he probably wouldn't have called me, I wouldn't have had the opportunity to extend an invitation to you, and we wouldn't be having lunch today." Her laughter tinkled like the ice in her second drink. "So, maybe I should thank Liza."

Lona slid the salad plates and a basket of tiny biscuits onto the table.

"I'm curious about why she would be so upset at not hearing from her father." Samantha bit into a biscuit light as air. "Didn't George say something about a family tradition of betting on ball games?"

Lona moved to a side table and stood there rearranging some already perfectly arranged flowers.

"Oh, they've been doing that since she was practically a baby," Queen answered. "You know how men are, always want their firstborn to be a boy." She lowered her voice the way Southern women always do when they talk about childbirth, one of their favorite topics. "And when it turned out that Liza was to be our only child, such a *difficult* delivery, I think Forrest encouraged her to be interested in boyish things."

"But surely he's missed calling her on a Saturday morning before."

"Of course! I think Liza's a little hysterical these days. She recently broke off with her boyfriend." Queen smiled. "You know how young love is."

"Yes, of course. And where did you say Forrest is? Away on business?"

Queen turned to the sideboard, where Lona was still standing. "Lona, did you forget something?"

"No'm, I was just straightening this table," she said, and then evaporated.

Queen smiled. "Aren't we forever at the mercy of

our help? I swear, I think Lona would quit if she couldn't snoop into all my business."

Sam nodded, wondering what Queen's business was. "Did you say Forrest was in San Francisco?"

"Why, yes, he is. He's been there over a week. Such a *lovely* city. Do you miss it?"

"Sometimes." Determined not to let Queen sidetrack her, she pushed for details. "Lovely hotels, too. What's Forrest's favorite?"

Queen turned to her with wide blue eyes. "Why, I don't rightly believe I know. *Mine* is the Stanford Court. Mr. Nassikas there always remembers Forrest and me from when we used to stay with him in New Orleans at the Royal Orleans. We get *such* grand treatment. But Forrest doesn't stay there when he's on business." She took a long pull on her drink and set it down emphatically on the tabletop. She was about to change the subject again. "Now, tell me," she said, turning and placing a hand on Sam's arm, "why you never married and had children."

Sam wrote a question in her mental notebook—Why *wouldn't* Queen tell her where Ridley was staying?—then answered, "I *was* married, when I was very young."

"Well, it's still not too late for you to have children. You don't know what you're missing."

"I'm sure you're right—about what I'm missing. But I'm 'aunt' to lots of friends' children. I'm afraid I never would have been very good in the bad times. I like children when they're dry and cute—and for about an hour. Then I want to give them back."

Queen laughed. "No, little girls aren't *all* sugar and spice."

"Not even Liza?"

"Oh, goodness no. I mean, *we* think she's perfect, of course, because she's ours, but she always has been a *different* child."

"Difficult?" Then Sam bit her tongue. What the hell was she doing? She knew no mother was going to come clean on her offspring. And implying criticism was no way to find out.

"Heavens, no! Just toodles along to a different drummer. But she's doing beautifully at Agnes Scott even though she wanted to go away to school. She's a painter, you know."

"What would have been her first choice?"

"Of schools? Probably Parsons, or anywhere else in New York. The child is *crazy* about New York. She even looks like a New Yorker. Have you spent much time there?"

"I've visited it often. But why—"

Then Queen firmly steered the conversation once again onto travel, where it stayed until they finished lunch.

After her third drink, Queen excused herself and pushed back from the table. "There's a powder room down that hall." She gestured. "I'll be back in just a minute."

Sam sat stirring her iced tea with a silver spoon. Then she lifted the long-stemmed spoon and turned it over. Tiffany. Of course.

"May I give you some more?"

Sam jumped. She hadn't heard Lona enter the room. She nodded.

Lona poured the tea from the pitcher she was carrying, then stood motionless. She gave Sam a long look, and in that moment Sam could see a decision being settled upon.

"Miss Liza is *not* hysterical." She spoke so softly Sam could barely hear her. "She is the sanest child I've ever known."

Sam whispered back, for at any moment Queen might walk back into the room. "Then you think she has reason to be worried about her father?"

"If *she* thinks she does, she—" And then her voice rose. "Oglethorpe! Get out!" A rangy Dalmation bounded in. He ignored Lona's hissed reprimand and leaned his front paws on Sam's skirt.

"Down, boy!" she said, laughing. Oglethorpe gave her a wet kiss, then retreated.

"That dog's a mess!" Lona said, but Sam could tell she didn't really mean it. "He's always so bad, underfoot every time I turn around, 'specially when Mr. Ridley's away."

"He's especially attached to his master?"

"He's attached to anybody who'll put up with him. But Mr. Ridley, he takes Ogle for a long walk every night, walks with this big galoof running along beside." Lona laughed. "They *are* a sight!"

"Nobody else walks him?"

"I do, but he goes too fast for me. And he wants to go too far, always in the same direction Mr. Ridley walks him." She gestured over her shoulder in the vicinity of Piedmont Park. "I can't be every night walking all over hill and dale. I've got other things to study than that dog."

"Like bringing us some of your delicious lime sherbet for dessert," Queen said as she glided back into the room, placed one hand lightly on Lona's shoulder, and turned her heading out so that she had no choice but to go. Sam had seen less graceful moves

50

on the dance floor. Queen might not have a career, Sam thought, but she was a pro.

A quarter hour more of polite chitchat followed. Queen poured coffee from an antique silver service (most definitely the kind hidden from the Yankees) then managed to squeeze Sam's hand as she handed her the cup. "There now. Haven't we had the loveliest visit?"

Which meant, Sam knew, *Enough of this tête à tête. Drink up and get out.*

Sam smiled and muttered all the right things: enjoyed it . . . how nice . . . beautiful house . . . have you over soon. Then the two women brushed cheeks, and Sam went home.

She couldn't remember ever having been patted and touched so much by another human being and yet left so cold.

Three

◆

"THAT'S BULLSHIT," LIZA RIDLEY SAID FLATLY.

"Then you wouldn't characterize your parents' relationship as ideal?"

"I would characterize it as miserable." Liza gestured with both hands, her small, stubby fingers stuck straight out on the Formica tabletop.

Samantha and Liza Ridley were sharing an order of ketchup-doused french fries and sipping fountain cherry colas at Horton's, the coffee shop cum department/drug/bookstore on Oxford Road just across the street from Emory.

Sam had smiled when Liza suggested the meeting place, for she'd spent many happy hours in Horton's during her own youth, browsing through the jumble of merchandise that ranged from notebooks to mops to makeup, gossiping with friends, writing papers in between hamburgers and Cokes perhaps in this very booth.

When Uncle George had suggested the night before that Sam might want to give Liza a call, she'd protested that she wasn't spending her entire day on a young girl's imaginary problem. But after talking with Queen, she'd found herself stopping in a phone booth on Juniper and dialing Liza's number at Agnes Scott.

Damn you, George, she thought. He knew that between her sense of obligation (even if it were *his* obligation) and her curiosity, she'd make that phone call. Liza had been eager. She was at Horton's in fifteen minutes.

Sam inspected the petite young woman on the other side of the booth. Liza Ridley at twenty-one was a beauty—not an orthodox burst of Southern blondness, but small, with long dark hair, a pale complexion, blue eyes, and a heart-shaped face. Her mother was right about one thing: dressed from head to toe in black, Liza did look as if she'd be more at home on the streets of New York's punk East Village.

When Sam asked about her work, Liza had pulled a plastic envelope of slides from her voluminous black leather bag. The pieces they showed were collages of photographs of frogs, whales, and huge fish cut from magazines and pieced together with heroic swirls of paint. The themes were birth, death, sex, transfiguration. There was a lot more than met the eye to *this* little brunette, Sam thought.

"They're absolutely miserable with one another," Liza was saying. "I *know* why Queen hangs in there. She'd be nowhere without my father."

"Money?"

"Everything. She'd be *nothing* without him."

"Well, she'd keep the house, wouldn't she, and her friends?" But Sam knew she was playing the devil's advocate. She knew what Liza was going to say. She just wanted to hear her say it.

Liza laughed. "You've forgotten how it works in Atlanta. She *is* who my dad is. And if she doesn't have him, forget it. I've seen it happen with her friends. I've heard her talk about it. And it doesn't even have to be divorce. Her friend Marjorie—nine months after her husband's heart attack, she killed herself with an overdose of sleeping pills."

"From grief?"

"From loneliness. From being frozen out. For women like Queen—"

Sam couldn't help but interrupt. "Do you always call your mother Queen?"

"Ever since she asked me to, when I was three years old." Liza smiled an odd smile, leaned her head back, and dropped a ketchup-covered french fry into her mouth from above. "Anyway, nobody ever invited Marjorie anywhere again, except to lunch. But never to dinner parties with the men, or to house parties in the summer up at Tate or at the lake. And never on couples trips."

"Why?"

"Because she didn't have a husband anymore who was part of the group."

"So she'd lost her passport."

Liza nodded.

"And no one offered to fix her up with another man?"

"They were too afraid she was going to steal one of theirs."

"What about someone new, from the outside?"

Sam knew the answer to that, too. There was no new blood in the old circle. You could buy yourself the biggest house in Atlanta with new money, but that wouldn't get you into the club.

Liza gave her an incredulous look. "What planet are you from?"

Samantha laughed. "I *do* know what you're talking about. I think that, subconsciously, that's one of the reasons I left Atlanta—or at least, why I stayed away so long."

Liza looked at her. "I'm leaving, too, when I finish school. I can't believe you came back."

"Well, it's a long story. But let's get back to your mother's friend Marjorie."

"She could do whatever she wanted to. No one cared anymore, see? That's the point. But she wouldn't *want* to. She'd been *inside,* and you don't get more inside in this city than being married to a partner at Simmons and Lee. After that, it's all downhill."

"A doctor wouldn't do—a banker?"

"Nope. Might as well be *black.*" Liza said that last word in an ironic way that told Sam about her liberal posture.

"Okay. So we know why Queen wouldn't divorce your father. But what about him? And what makes you think they're so miserable in the first place?"

"Which one do you want answered?"

Sam shrugged. "Both."

"I have to tell you about him. Forrest Ridley is the most wonderful man in the world."

Sam laughed a little. "Lots of daughters think that, Liza, if you'll pardon me for saying so."

"But he is! He's funny, and he's kind. He's always there when I need him." Her face clouded. She looked up at Sam, and suddenly her eyes were glistening with the threat of tears.

For the first time, Sam saw the little girl within the

young woman. She reached over and patted Liza's hand. "Go on."

"My friends tease me about being a daddy's girl, and they say I'm spoiled. But I'm not. Daddy's never spoiled me. He's given me lots of advantages, I know that. And I'm grateful for them. But he's always talked with me as if I'm a real person, not just his child. He taught me to respect people, to look for the good in them, and then to allow them their differences—just like he's allowed me mine."

"You're a little different from the other girls you know?"

Liza smiled at the understatement. "You might say so. But Daddy didn't stand in the way of my doing what I wanted, of my becoming a painter instead of a debutante."

"Ah-ha! I knew we had something in common."

"You paint, too?"

"No, I told them to take all that coming-out routine and shove it."

"You did? Truly?"

"Truly."

Liza leaned forward as if they were the closest of girlfriends sharing a confidence sweet as a chocolate ice cream sundae. "While the other girls in my group were going to New York to buy their dresses for their balls, I flew to New York too and stayed for a month with Daddy's sister, my Aunt Jean, who's in advertising, and we did all the galleries. And then she took me for another month abroad. I saw *everything!*" She burbled on. "The Louvre, Giverny, the Prado, the Sistine Chapel, the châteaux."

"Some dad to let you do that. And Queen?"

"Shit a brick. Said I'd ruined my life and that

Daddy had helped me. She didn't speak to either of us for months." She paused. "They don't talk much at home anyway. They've slept in separate bedrooms for years."

Samantha thought about the house tour Queen had taken her on. They'd skipped the family quarters on the second floor. Was Queen touchy about the number of occupied bedrooms?

"If you saw them in public, you'd never guess," Liza continued. "They're all lovey-dovey, or at least Queen is, and Daddy doesn't do anything to change that impression and embarrass her."

"Do you like your mother?"

The young woman didn't miss a beat. "No, not very much. She's not very likable. Did you think so?"

Sam hesitated. She was notorious for her directness, but in this case, she wondered, shouldn't she try . . .

Liza laughed at her hesitation. "Your Uncle George told me I'd like you. He said we're a lot alike."

"He's right. No, I don't like Queen, Liza. I think she's one cold customer."

Liza said softly, as if she were talking to herself, "I've always thought of her as the Ice Queen."

"So why does your father stick?"

"I've asked him that very thing."

Samantha looked into the blue of Liza's direct gaze. She wouldn't want it trained on her when coupled with such a question.

"He always just shakes his head and says that promises like 'till death do us part' are promises not lightly undertaken."

"Tell me why you're so worried about him now," Sam said.

Once again Sam heard about how Liza and her father had a standing date to bet the ball games every weekend.

"Queen says he's missed dates with you before," she said when Liza paused.

"Never."

"And that you've forgotten that fact because you're upset about breaking up with your boyfriend."

"Really? Now, isn't that interesting. I don't have a boyfriend. I've never had a serious boyfriend in my whole life."

Four

───────◆───────

WHAT'S FOR SUPPER?" SAM ASKED, WALKING through the kitchen.

Peaches was standing at the butcher-block work-table in the middle of the room, stirring cornmeal batter. "Nothing for you. Horace and I are having some hot tamale pie, but George said you all are eating out, going to a party."

"George!" Sam called down the hall as she wheeled out of the kitchen and headed toward his private quarters. She stalked through the open door of his sitting room.

"I waste my whole day talking with *your* friends about *their* problems, and then I come home to have Peaches inform me I'm going to a party! What the hell is going on here?"

George looked at her with perfect equanimity. "It's nearly dusk. You must have enjoyed yourself if you stayed so long." He reached over and turned down the volume on the recording of a book he was

59

listening to on his new state-of-the-art sound system. "This new Le Carré is something. Have you read it?"

"I asked you a question."

"I like it almost better than the Smileys."

She was exasperated. "Yes, I loved the book. And yes, I enjoyed talking to Liza, and Queen Ridley is some piece of work. No, I did not spend the entire day with them; I did manage to scratch out two or three cents' worth of a livelihood by meeting with Hoke, and after seeing Liza I went back to the morgue and read background on sheriffs for a couple of hours. Though there's been precious little in the news. I think I've already exhausted it. These boys aren't much for publicity."

"That's probably why you're so cranky. Not that I didn't warn you. And they're not going to be any more welcoming when you come snooping around, either."

"That is *not* what we're talking about. We're talking about this damned party you think I'm going to. You know I don't do parties."

"And Peaches and Horace don't do windows. Never did. I have to bring in a service."

"What does that have to do with the price of raddicchio at Cloudt's Market?"

George grinned. "I thought you might want to meet some of Forrest Ridley's friends. Edison Kay, one of the partners, is giving a cocktail party tonight. I didn't mention it before because you're such a stick-in-the-mud about social gatherings, but since it's a perfect opportunity . . ." He trailed off.

Sam spoke to the ceiling. "Why do I take this

abuse? Is it because when I got sober I discovered that no one ever says anything interesting after ten o'clock —and that nobody says anything interesting at cocktail parties *before* ten o'clock either?" She shifted her focus to George. *"Why* do you think I want to meet Ridley's friends?"

"Because you're curious about the man." George twinkled. "We don't have to stay long. Maybe Ridley will even be back from wherever he's been by then and will show up at the party, and Liza's worries will all be for naught. We'll have a handful of fabulous hors d'oeuvres and come home."

"While I'm still hungry?" Sam snorted. "That's the other thing I hate about these damned parties. I end up starving. You can't eat a proper meal while you're standing around talking, and you can't have a decent conversation because you're so busy working the room."

"Peaches is making enough tamale pie for leftovers," George said. "Or we can probably twist Horace's arm to stop us by the Varsity on the way home."

Sam considered that offer for a minute. As much a part of the fabric of Atlanta as the Dogwood Festival, the Varsity was a gigantic drive-in and sit-down chili dog, french fry, and onion ring emporium near Georgia Tech that did so much business it had a glass-walled room devoted solely to the chopping of onions. Sam and Horace were mad about it. Peaches, who sneered at all cooking other than her own, was convinced the place served up sudden death.

"Okay," Sam said begrudgingly. "But I'm only

doing it to humor you. We're staying one hour. And we *better* stop at the Varsity."

Samantha wasn't dressed like a woman who was going to get a chili dog as she walked out the back door on the arm of her uncle. She was wearing a black silk slip of a dress with tiny sparkling rhinestones marching up and down its spaghetti straps. The dress was cut low enough to show off her considerable cleavage. Her color was high, her mouth a slash of scarlet. Her halo of short springy curls glistened like the regularly waxed finish of George's old black Lincoln.

"You going to be warm enough, Sam?" Horace asked as he tucked her and George into the back seat.

"I brought a shawl," she said, and held up a length of black cashmere with openwork like lace. Horace smiled, for Peaches had admired this shawl so much that Sam had ordered her one like it from San Francisco, except that Peaches' wrap was the green of an old glass Coke bottle, perfect with her golden-brown complexion.

Horace straightened the bill of his favorite Atlanta Braves cap in the mirror, then wheeled the ancient Lincoln around the side of the house on the winding brick drive.

"Mr. Kay's?" he asked, confirming their destination, and then they were on their way—hell-bent for leather, which was how Horace always drove. He was a superb navigator of the city's roundabout routes and curving byways, which he considered a huge race-course, and knew every inch of Atlanta except the new suburbs—which, in his opinion, didn't matter anyway.

"So you thought Queen was cold," George remarked.

"Glacial," said Sam. "But Liza says her father's a real winner. Is he?"

"Yep. But Forrest Ridley's always been a puzzlement to me, too. He's a real Jack Armstrong, all-American. As clean-cut as they come. The right schools. *Law Review.* We recruited him as an intern, the summer between his second and third years of University of Virginia law school. He's always pulled more than his load, brought in millions in billable business. Made partner right on schedule, and has been an asset to the firm since the day he came on board."

"So what's the puzzlement?"

"I always wonder about anyone who has a permanent smile on his face."

"Makes you wonder what you'd see if that smile ever cracked, doesn't it?" Horace interjected from the front seat. "I bet he wasn't so happy about that party at his house."

"What's that?" George asked.

"Said I bet Mr. Ridley was upset about that surprise party at his house a time ago."

"What party?" asked George. "You been holding out on me?"

George was referring to Horace's position as a major operator in the underground telegraph of gossip that connected the household help of the city's Four Hundred. In fact, more than once in his law practice, George had depended upon that telegraph, for the word of a well-placed cook or housekeeper was better than that of a paid snitch, and the information thus gained was rich and substantial rather than a few dry facts that might only scratch the surface of the truth.

"I guess I forgot. But anyway," said Horace, settling into the beginning of the story as if he were settling into an easy chair, "what I heard was that one evening a few weeks ago, all these people in black tie started showing up at Ridley's front door, but he and Miz Queen weren't expecting them."

"How many?" George asked.

"Well . . ." Horace pushed back his cap a bit. "Before it was all over, there were about a hundred and fifty."

"That many!" Sam exclaimed. "And they weren't invited?"

"Oh, they were invited, all right. It was just that the Ridleys didn't do the inviting. Didn't know anyone else had done it for them, either. They were just sitting around the house on a Thursday night, I think it was, in their pj's watching the TV when the first ones arrived."

"I don't understand," said Sam.

"They didn't either. Seems what happened was that *somebody* sent out a whole bunch of engraved invitations, said it was a surprise party for Mr. Ridley, so there was no RSVP."

"What did they do?" George asked.

"Best they could. Jumped up and got dressed—I hear it was the fastest Miz Queen ever got herself together in her life." Horace chuckled. "Then they called all over town to restaurants where they're known and had them send over platters of hors d'oeuvres quick as they could."

"So they were good sports about it," said Samantha.

"Well, I wouldn't go that far. They pulled it off, and I guess by the time about half the guests had arrived, the newcomers wouldn't have known what a surprise it really was, if the others hadn't told 'em. But after it was over, I heard Miz Queen had a fit. A real hissy. Said it was all Mr. Ridley's fault—someone making a fool of her."

"Well, well, well," George said. "Isn't that something?"

Horace careened the old Lincoln, tires squealing, off Peachtree onto Andrews Road. In moments they would be at their destination.

"Any theories about who sent those invitations?" Sam asked.

Horace, who was concentrating on passing a delivery van, shook his head.

They zipped past palatial estates, each of them set far back from the road behind a carefully manicured park. In this North Side neighborhood of Andrews and Habersham and West Paces Ferry roads, above the springtime fragrance of lilac and wisteria floated the aroma of old money.

Then they were at the Kays' gate, where a young college boy in a white jacket greeted them. "Good to see you this evening, Mr. Adams, Ms. Adams," he said.

George grinned at Samantha's surprise. "Edison never does things halfway."

"Does he have mug books?" she asked.

As another young man handed them out of the car under the porte cochere, Horace, who would park the car and then wait for them in a back room where a poker game had probably already started, leaned out the window.

"I'll nose around and see what I can find out about those invitations," he said.

"You just concentrate on winning," Sam called behind her. "Then it's the Varsity, guys. My treat. Or depending on what you take the suckers for, Horace, yours."

Five

◆

EDISON KAY STOOD IN HIS BLACK-AND-WHITE MARBLE-tiled foyer with arms spread wide. A tall, sub-stantial, fiftyish man with wings of gray in the dark brown hair that he wore long in the old-fashioned planter/politician style, Kay cut an impressive figure.

"George!" he cried. "Why, it's been a month of Sundays since I've seen you. *Delighted* that you could make it. Though I wouldn't give a hoot about you coming if I hadn't wanted to rest my eyes on the beautiful Miss Samantha." He laughed expansively, and Sam found herself being gathered up and smoth-ered in a bear hug that smelled of lemony Guerlain 4711 and bourbon.

Then he pulled back, smiling into her face while still holding her by the shoulders. His was a handsome face, clean-shaven, with a long aristocratic nose and brown eyes that were knowing but not particularly warm.

"Why, I haven't seen you since you were fourteen

or fifteen years old. I'd heard tell that you were back from Baghdad-by-the-Bay, having transmogrified yourself from a young colt into a full-fledged woman, but your Uncle George has been keeping you well hidden."

Sam didn't remember ever having seen this golden-tongued man in her entire life, but then George was saying something about going up to the Kays' house in Tate one summer, and she smiled politely and said, "It's good to see you again, too."

"Hell!" Edison laughed. "No need to be so formal." He dropped one arm down to Sam's waist. "Kay Kay, come see who's done us the honor."

Edison Kay's wife—whose Christian name made her Kay Kay, which she was always called as if she were named Billie Sue or Mary Ann or one of those other double-barreled Southernisms—was as blond as Queen Ridley and of about the same stature. But there the resemblance ended, for Kay Kay hailed from Fort Worth, and her good-old-Texas-girl voice projected across her foyer as easily as it did across a cow lot.

"Why, hon," she said to Samantha, "I'm so glad to see you I could hug your neck." And then she did so, landing a kiss on Sam's left ear in the process. "Now, you just come with me." She took Sam's hand and pulled her away from Edison. "He's just a dirty old man, baby, who doesn't have your best interests at heart. But I'm going to introduce you to every handsome man in this house."

And it was *some* house. A copy of an antebellum Alabama planter's mansion that had been on the Kay side of the family, the graceful whitewashed brick and columned structure rose to three stories, connected inside by twin staircases. The living room seemed to go on forever, with a dozen conversational areas—blue, gold, and white sofas and chairs grouped around glass tables that held crystal bowls in which magnolias floated. Across the far wall, a series of french doors led onto a brick terrace. The room buzzed with the chatter of a party already in full swing, occasionally punctuated by a bright bugle of sound as two women greeted one another, or the leonine roar that marked the end of a well-told dirty joke.

"Your home is beautiful," Sam said to Kay Kay, meaning the compliment.

"Fifteen thousand heated square feet," Kay Kay said, and laughed.

Sam turned and looked at her. Kay Kay's smile was blindingly white. Sam was suddenly reminded of all those shiny Texas girls who won beauty contests—something in the genes, something in the water.

"Ed tries to keep me from saying things like that, but, honey, you just can't stop a Texas girl from bragging." Kay Kay paused a second and tugged her wine-colored silk bodice down over her generous bosom. "God, am I parched. What do you have to do to get a drink around this joint?"

At that moment, a waiter carrying a silver tray filled with tulip-shaped glasses of champagne appeared. Behind him was another waiter serving little biscuits filled with Virginia ham and miniature croissants stuffed with crab salad.

Kay Kay picked off a glass for each of them. Sam held hers politely, biding her time until she could abandon it for some club soda. Kay Kay slugged the wine right down. No doubt about it: well before the evening was over, Kay Kay was going to be a goner.

Sam looked around the room. "Who *are* all those people?"

Kay Kay burst into laughter. "'Swhat I like, a woman who wants to know something and just asks it." She surveyed the crowd for a minute, narrowing her eyes as if she'd never seen any of them before. She grinned. "Weird-looking bunch of sons-of-bitches, ain't it? My B list. Not *you*, of course, darlin'"—a line which, Sam knew, she would repeat twenty times before the evening was over—"but a lot of these folks are here just for professional reasons. Course, we almost always mix business and pleasure, 'cause S and L is our life, but at a big do like this we ask clients and judges and a passel of others."

"Judges?"

"Sure, honey." Kay Kay turned and looked at her. "Why not?"

"I never knew the bench fraternized with lawyers."

"Well, they're not exactly the enemy, you know," Kay Kay said with a hearty Texas laugh, then pointed at a very short, stocky man who was holding a champagne glass in each hand while he gazed squarely into the cleavage of a tall redhead. "That's Judge Deaver. Now, would you begrudge him that bubbly or those boobs?"

Sam chuckled along with her hostess, who laughed at all her own lines. Well, now, wasn't this interesting?

"Maybe you'll get to meet our daughter, Totsie," Kay Kay was saying as she reached for another glass of champagne from a passing tray. "Or maybe not. She's upstairs hiding."

"The shy retiring type?"

"Hell, no. Totsie's about as shy as I am. Even when she was a little bit of a thing, she was always leading cheers or twirling her baton or shooting her little rifle. She's loud like me. *Likes* a lot of noise. Likes to be noticed, too. Her sole ambition in life is to be beamed into every living room in America—to be Jane Pauley. She's working on it right now, getting paid about two cents an hour working for Turner Broadcasting."

Sam was confused. "You mean she's working tonight?"

"Nah." Kay Kay gestured toward the stairs with her glass. "She's up there in her room getting over a fight with her boyfriend, Trey. She's been crying for two days. I told her to slap some cold tea bags over those eyes and get her little tail down here."

Just then, as if her mother's wish were her command, Totsie Kay materialized on the stairs. She was a fresh-scrubbed young blonde in golden-pink silk. Small, but rounded in all the right places, she looked like a dish of peach ice cream. Totsie flashed her mother a smile that was a bit nervous but nonetheless, like her mother's, almost blinding in its porcelain whiteness.

"Honey, I'm so glad you're feeling better." Kay Kay took Totsie by the arm as if she were a little girl in her pinafore to be pushed forward. "Now, *this* is Samantha Adams. I know you two have lots to talk about. I'll see you both later." With that, Kay Kay exchanged her empty glass for a full one from the tray of a passing waiter. So much for being introduced to every handsome man in the room, Sam thought wryly. *"Fenster!* You old dog!" Kay Kay cried to an approaching guest, and trailed off.

Samantha turned back to the daughter, who was still smiling brightly.

71

"I follow your byline in the paper," Totsie said, so softly that Sam had to lean toward her. Was her mother kidding? This sweet young thing a cheerleader? In television? "That was a super series you did on the election scandal. I've been wanting to meet you." Totsie was picking up speed as she went along, and her voice was growing louder. "Daddy said that since you were George's niece, sooner or later he'd wangle an introduction for me."

"Why, I'm flattered," Sam said, and she was.

"Actually, really, I mean . . . I thought," Totsie stammered, "one day I'd run into you at a Women's Club luncheon. I mean, Press Club," she corrected herself, frowning, "Women's Press Club." And then she spilled champagne down the front of her pretty dress. "Oh, shit!" Her lip trembled. "Will you excuse me?"

Before Sam could respond, Totsie evaporated. She fled back up the stairs down which she'd come.

The girl certainly wasn't feeling well, Sam thought. She looked positively feverish. If at her age she was letting a fight with her boyfriend get to her this badly, she was going to have miles of bad road ahead. But then, Sam reminded herself, think how badly she herself had let Beau Talbot . . . She shook her head.

Perish the thought of Beau Talbot.

Sam had had a very high incidence of coincidence in her life. It was almost as if she could conjure up people. She thought of them, and then—

"Excuse me."

Oh, God! She whirled. But the handsome frown at her elbow was very young and unfamiliar.

The frown's owner bowed slightly. "I'm Trey Nelson. Did I just see you talking with Totsie?"

"Yes, you did." Sam's sigh of relief made his frown deepen. She pointed toward the stairs. "But she spilled her drink and went up to change."

Young Nelson excused himself again, ran his hand through his dark red curls, and wheeled, almost bumping into a waiter.

This was *some* lovers' quarrel. Both of them looked shattered.

Two women passed, their arms intertwined. "Well, who *knew* where he was from? So I said, 'Why, I don't believe I know his daddy.'"

Which meant the person in question could have been born of a white trash banjo picker and a she-wolf, for all the welcome he was going to get.

More waiters waltzed by bearing piles of boiled shrimp and red sauce for dunking. Conversation buzzed all around, but none of it lit on Sam. She wished she were home. She could be eating Peaches' hot tamale pie, or snuggling with Harpo on her chaise, reading.

Well, she couldn't just stand here. If she kept moving, it would *look* as if she were mingling.

And then, before she knew it, she was.

"Aren't you George Adams's niece, Samantha?" a woman asked as she passed a group gathered beneath a family portrait of the Kays. Wives of Simmons & Lee partners, they made a space in their circle for her and continued their talk. The topic was the opening of summer houses in the firm's informal compound in Tate.

"It gets so musty during the winter," a brunette in

red was saying. "I've got to get Elspeth and her son up there to give it a good cleaning."

"Is she staying the season? I just can't get Corrine to stay."

"I know what you mean, darling, though since May's husband died she's more willing. But you, with all those children—maybe I can get May to come over and give you a hand from time to time."

"I sure would appreciate it."

Suddenly the devil grabbed Sam's tongue. "It must be hard for them up there," she said, as if she didn't know better.

Polite eyes rolled her way. "Why, whatever do you mean?"

"Well, isn't Tate in Forsyth County? Where all those Klan marches and demonstrations were last year?"

A silence fell upon the group. Silk shifted. Champagne slipped between pursed lips.

"Why, no, actually, Tate's in Pickens County," said a redhead in pea green.

"But it's more or less the same, isn't it? I mean, all white? It must be uncomfortable for your help to be there." Even as she spoke, Sam wondered at herself. Wasn't she the perfect flaming liberal twit? What the hell was she doing? Just bored—cruising for a fight, looking for a hit? She was going to have to talk about this at a meeting: bitchery—an alternative to alcohol.

"I never thought of it like that," the brunette said. "But then, our help stays with us, you know. It's not as if they're out gallivanting all over the countryside."

"Tell us about San Francisco, Samantha," interjected a silver-haired woman with a massive bosom battened down beneath plum silk. The mediator. "It is the most *beautiful* city. I can't imagine why you'd want to come back to little old Atlanta after living there."

And they were off and running, expounding on California's charms. Queen had done exactly the same thing. It was as if this set had agreed on travelogues as a sort of salve, a vanishing cream for confrontation.

"Look at those girls," said a woman with a frizzy brown permanent. She tipped her head to one side like a listening bird. "Don't they remind you of flowers?"

They did look that pretty, the nearby cluster of young girls in their bright party dresses. Their complexions were as creamy as Kay Kay's magnolias. More than one of the women in Sam's group fluttered an age-freckled hand to her throat.

A blonde in blue watered silk caught Sam's eye, and smiled. It was Totsie, changed into a fresh dress. She came over.

"Come join us." She took Sam's hand. "I want you to meet some of my friends."

Sam let herself be led away, and a collective sigh of relief rose from the women she left behind her.

". . . didn't mean to be rude," Totsie was saying. "After all, I *am* a hostess."

She looked better now, though her eyes were too bright. Was she on something? Sam wondered.

Totsie introduced her around the circle of animated young women.

"San Francisco!" one of them shrieked. "I *love* that city!"

"Oh, I *died* over the cable cars."

"The foghorns," mooned one who had the slow eyes of a poet.

"Oh, you *would,* Ashley," Totsie twitted her friend. "Now, *my* favorite is the view from the top of the Mark Hopkins."

"You've stayed there?" Sam asked.

"No, but I had drinks there once."

"Totsie is *so* sophisticated," one of them teased.

She was right, Samantha thought. For despite the fact that the Kays' daughter was obviously having a bad night, there was something very grown-up about her. She was no little girl in a pinafore, Sam thought, no simple, sweet confection.

"Totsie's going to be the head of Turner Broadcasting one of these days," another offered. "Going to push Ted Turner right out."

"Over his dead body," said Totsie. Her color was high, her skin so pale that the blood showed like bright stains in her cheeks. She laughed, took a gulp of champagne, and then started to choke.

Samantha patted her on the back. Totsie *was* having a rough time with the bubbly. Her color deepened. Sam considered the Heimlich maneuver, but instead reached for a sandwich from a nearby table.

"Here," she said. "The bread will help."

Totsie chewed and swallowed, then again. "Thanks," she finally managed in a strained voice. "I'll be okay."

One of the girls turned to another, as if to politely draw attention away from Totsie. "Where's Liza tonight?" she asked.

"Probably painting. She hardly ever comes to these things anymore. Always says she's too busy."

How many Lizas could there be in their circle? "Liza Ridley?" asked Sam.

"You know her?"

"I've met her. Saw some of her work. She's quite good."

The girls nodded all around.

"She's super," one said.

"She is," a girl with dark bangs agreed. "When we were little kids, at Westminster"—she tilted her head in the direction of that very private school, farther out on West Paces Ferry Road—"Liza's work was up in every show." She laughed. "That Liza! I remember one summer when we were all up at Tate, Liza must have been eight or nine, and she had a whole bunch of us posing out on a rock in the lake, buck naked! Big Helen, my mama, caught us and threw a hissy. They thought we were playing doctor."

"Playing what?" asked a young girl as she joined the circle. "Are you all talking about my daddy again?"

"No, Beth. We're talking about Liza."

Samantha turned to look at the newcomer named Beth, and then it was *her* turn to choke.

No question. This beauty was Beau Talbot's daughter. With her dark hair, long elegant nose, and big long-lashed brown eyes, the girl was a female version of the young doctor who had taken Sam's love.

"Samantha Adams, Beth Talbot." Totsie was doing the honors.

When Sam touched the girl's hand, her own tingled.

Beth smiled. Her front teeth were just a little crooked, charmingly so, like her father's. "My dad's mentioned you."

Oh, yeah?

"He always reads you in the paper. He says you're

77

the best reporter the *Constitution*'s ever had. He says—oh, here he is now."

Sam closed her eyes. If she could conjure him up, she could conjure him away.

"Samantha!" There was his voice, the same surprisingly high voice with a laugh permanent-pressed into it.

He was bald. She knew he was going to be bald. He was fat. His teeth had gone bad. His face was a moonscape of valleys and wrinkles.

She opened her eyes. He was infuckingcredibly gorgeous.

He was grinning at her. *Grinning.* "Samantha, you're just as beautiful as ever." Then he laughed.

The circle of girls disappeared. So did the rest of the room.

"You haven't changed," she managed to say. She felt like she was going to explode. The last time she'd seen this bastard, she'd been nineteen years old. He'd kissed her good-bye at the airport—kissed her again and again. "It won't be long," he'd whispered in that high voice that broke. "You'll come to New York." Then he'd held her one last time and whispered into her curls, "I'll love you always."

Shit! He might as well have said, "Let's have lunch." But nineteen-year-old girls didn't know that meant the same thing as "Let's be friends" or "I'll call you." Girls were usually women by the time they figured out that's what men said when they meant "Adios."

"Well . . ." He laughed and ran a hand across the top of his thatch of hair, which *had* changed—from black to silver. Gorgeous silver. "I'd beg to differ with you."

"Nawh," she said, sounding like a Dead End Kid. "You haven't changed a bit."

His eyes shifted a little at that, as if he weren't sure what she meant. He was off balance. Great.

"So. How do you like the *Constitution?*"

"So far, so good." She was volunteering nothing. He wanted to know how the last twenty years had gone? Let him ask.

"They're treating you nicely down there?"

"Yep. Sure are."

"You're not going to talk to me, are you?"

"Nope."

"Come on, Sam." He reached for her arm.

She shrugged away from him. "Please don't."

The truth was, if he touched her, she didn't know what she'd do. Cry. Scream. Detonate. She'd had a hate-on for this man for so many years, and now that she'd finally laid eyes on him again . . . what? What was this she felt?

Nervous. That's it.

That's not it. Try another four-letter word.

Hate.

No, you said that.

Anger.

Too many letters.

Fear.

That's warmer. That's partially right. And why do you fear him? What are you afraid of? What do you *really* feel? Nervous actually was warm, too. Try twitchy.

Twitchy doesn't have four letters.

Neither does ants-in-your-pants, but that's what you feel.

I do not.

Do too.

You mean . . . I can't believe it . . . *lust?* This is not lust.

You can lie to them, babe, but you can't lie to me. For my money, it's lust. Heat. Same thing. Lust.

She'd always been a sucker for a pretty face. A pretty body. Pretty smile. Beau Talbot—cad, four-flusher, scoundrel, cheat, heartbreaker—had all three. Years, miles, water under the bridge—and still, just looking at him made her hot. This was not logic operating here. She wanted his body. She hated his guts.

But there were other people around. This was a party. She'd been raised a Southern lady, to be polite. She didn't throw her club soda in his face. She didn't walk away. And she didn't want to let him see that he was getting to her.

"They're treating me very nicely downtown," she said. "I have a lot of latitude."

He was anxious to make small talk. "Well, be careful. You know what they say about plenty of rope."

She smiled politely. "That's what George says. He's been warning me off a story I'm beginning—says it's too dangerous."

"What's that?"

"A look-see at rural sheriffs."

"I'd say he's right. They play hardball, those ole boys. I wouldn't mess with 'em, Sam. Why don't you stick to something safe, like murder? You do that awfully well."

She wouldn't ask him how he knew. "Thanks." She nodded.

"I've read—" he began, but then a white-jacketed waiter appeared at his side.

"Dr. Talbot, there's a phone call for you, sir. I hate to interrupt, but the man said it was urgent."

"Excuse me, Sam." And he did touch her then—just tapped her arm. It tingled as if she'd been shocked. "Please don't disappear. I'll be back in a minute."

She stood rooted, not thinking about what she ought to be doing: mingling, making conversation, or, if she had any sense, making tracks. Beau Talbot, after all these years. Her arm sent electric messages up, then down to her breast.

He returned quickly, wearing a very odd expression. But before either of them could say another word, Edison Kay stepped up.

"Well, well," Kay blustered around an expensive cigar. "How nice to see you getting to know some people, Samantha. Though I must say that, even though Dr. Talbot here's the handsomest dog in the room, he is that, a dog. You ought to be careful."

Beau smiled politely, then blurted, "Excuse me, Samantha, Edison, I've got to leave."

"Rushing out?" Edison protested. "Why, the party's only just begun."

Beau leaned over to his host and murmured in his ear, but loudly enough that Sam could hear him. "I just got a call from the GBI. They've found Forrest

Ridley's body at Apalachee Falls, up in Watkin County."

"What the hell do you mean, Forrest Ridley's body?" Edison exclaimed loudly. "The man's a senior partner. He can't be dead!"

And with that, the party froze, dead still. Champagne tulips stopped halfway to lips. Words were bitten half-through like cigars. Then the buzz began, and grew and grew until it was almost a roar, and in the midst of it, there was a sharper swell of noise as a woman screamed. George suddenly appeared at Sam's side, and she never did see who had uttered such an anguished, unladylike sound.

Six

———◆———

SAM JOLTED AWAKE AND, WITH HER EYES STILL CLOSED, slammed her hand down on the alarm clock on her bedside table. But it kept ringing. She peeled one eye open and stared at it. Seven A.M. Harpo glared at her from the foot of her bed. Still ringing. She fumbled for the telephone.

"Meet me at the IHOP on Ponce for breakfast," the voice on the other end said. "I have something important to tell you."

"Who *is* this?"

"Come on, Sam. It's Beau. Get up and get dressed and meet me."

"Are you crazy?"

"For Christ's sake, it's about Forrest Ridley. Don't you want this story?"

Sam was quiet for a moment as the events of the previous night played back through her mind like an old movie: the announcement of Ridley's death, the hubbub and confusion, the drive back home, skipping the Varsity. But she remembered too the way she'd felt when she'd seen Beau again—the confusion of all those years of hating him, blocking him, forgetting him, and then *zap!* he touched her, and that tingle.

"No."

"No what? No, you don't want this story? Or, no, you don't want breakfast at the IHOP?"

"None of it."

He paused. "Okay, you're right. The IHOP's a bad choice."

It was, for they'd eaten scores of blueberry pancakes there when they were lovers. The peaked-roof restaurant was filled with memories. Sam had avoided the chain ever since, even in San Francisco.

"How about the Silver Skillet?" he suggested.

"No."

"Gravy and biscuits, along with the skinny on Forrest Ridley? First dibs on what the Watkin County sheriff had to say? Wear your raincoat. It's pouring."

He was tempting her. But the Silver Skillet was another of their old haunts.

Then, as if he could read her mind, he said, "Melvin's, and that's my best offer."

"Where's Melvin's?"

She could hear his grin as he gave her directions.

"This had better be worth it."

In the parking lot Sam spotted what had to be Beau's car, a silver BMW with MD plates. Except for the color, it was a twin to hers. She frowned. The coincidence didn't please her.

As she ran for the front door, raindrops were dancing in the puddles.

Melvin's, on Northside Drive, had that look of

most of Atlanta's favorite breakfast hangouts: decorated with a medley of chrome and Formica, it was ramshackle, greasy, and seedy. But the biscuits were fluffy, the coffeepot bottomless, and you could order fresh pork loin, country or sugar-cured ham, a pork chop, or two kinds of sausage with your eggs, grits, and redeye gravy.

Beau stood at the counter talking with a waitress whose name tag declared her to be Bernice. He was dressed in a dark gray suit with a raincoat tossed over his shoulder. She hated the way he looked; he was absolutely, even first thing in the morning, beautiful. She was glad she'd just thrown on jeans, a bright red sweatshirt, and a matching smudge of lipstick. Let him see how little she cared about this meeting.

"God, you look wonderful," he said, turning as she approached. "I love the yellow slicker. Makes you look like a kid."

"Coffee, please," she said, looking straight at Bernice.

"Make that two." Beau took Sam's elbow and led her toward the last booth in the back corner.

She wondered if he often brought women here for breakfast. Was this his early morning hideaway? Or did he and what's-her-name, that woman from Boston he'd married, have a match made in heaven?

"So what was so important that you dragged me out of bed this lovely morning?" she demanded.

"The straight poop on Ridley," he said.

"What makes you think I care?"

"You're here. You're a reporter. You have a nose for murder. And you were already asking questions about him."

"How do you know that?"

Beau just smiled. His smiles always had been infuriating.

She shrugged. "Okay, I'm here. Shoot."

Even with his lights flashing and siren blaring, it had taken Beau an hour and a half to drive the seventy miles to Apalachee Falls State Park, where a hiker had found the body of Forrest Ridley. Route 400, the expressway, petered out north of Cumming, where he cut over to Route 19, and after that there was a maze of two-lane roads with ill-marked intersections and little towns with blinking red lights in their centers. The farther north he went, the more winding the roads and the slower his pace, for these were the foothills of the Appalachians. The 2,050-mile hiking trail, which stretched all the way to Maine, began at Springer Mountain just north of Apalachee.

It began to rain, but Beau had no trouble finding the entrance to the park; at its gate were two deputy sheriffs' cars, their revolving blue lights projecting an eerie lightshow across the deserted road. He flashed his identification, and the deputies waved him through with the slow, sly grin of the country lawman.

It was the kind of grin, Beau thought, that made you uneasy, encouraged worry about whether they only *thought* they knew more than city slickers, or really did. It was the kind of grin that made you feel that they were on the verge of writing you a speeding ticket and would make it stick, even if you'd been in your car sitting still.

The body had been found at the bottom of the falls, pinned beneath the overhang of a large flat rock. Lee Boggs, a kind-faced older man who was the Georgia

Bureau of Investigation's very best investigator, was already at work.

"Dr. Talbot." He nodded, pushing up his rain-spattered, rimless glasses.

"Boggs." Beau returned the nod. "What have we got here?"

"Well, not a hell of a lot. You can see what the terrain looks like." The creek was sheer on one side, edged with rocks and leaves on the other. "Course, if we're looking for footprints, I suspect they'd be up at the top anyway. I've got Masterson up there. But it's gonna be tough. You get a million hikers and campers up here with the first sign of good weather, and you know we had that more than a month ago. No telling how many people've tromped around here while he was lying in the water."

"Where the hell is the body?"

Boggs's cherubic face, more suited to a man selling lollipops than to one sifting through scenes of death, clouded over. "Sheriff took him. Said it was an open and shut case of accidental death, and hauled him right off to Monroeville."

"He *what!*"

"Sheriff Buford Dodd, his name was, said he didn't even know why we bothered to come up here anyway. Said the man obviously fell off the top of the falls and was killed. Said it's happened five or six times in the past ten years."

"Son-of-a-bitch!" Beau smacked his hand down on a rock, then shook it as if he was surprised at the pain. "Who called us, then? The sheriff do it just because the law says he's supposed to, even when he's not doing anything else by the book?"

"Don't know. I do know that we're probably not

going to learn much here. You might want to go on
down to Monroeville to the courthouse. Sheriff's
office is there. That's where they took him."

Beau turned away in disgust, heading back to his
car. Then he stopped. "Thanks, Boggs. Didn't mean
to blow up at you."

"'S okay, boss." The man grinned. "It's happened
before. Prob'ly happen again 'fore it's over."

It was nearing midnight when Beau got to the
Watkin County Sheriff's Office, part of a new blond-
brick county complex that had been built off to the
side of the old red courthouse, which stood squarely
in the middle of the road in the middle of town. Beau
hadn't had any dinner and had ruined a new pair of
shoes. His mood could be summarized as mean.

But he met his match in that category when he met
Buford Dodd. Not that the sheriff wasn't pleasant on
the surface—and neither was he hard on the eyes. He
stood level with Beau at six-foot-one, though he
outweighed the doctor's runner's body by a good forty
pounds, most of which was muscle packed in his
thighs, arms, and shoulders. Dark-haired, black-eyed,
with perhaps a touch of Cherokee blood somewhere
down the line, Buford Dodd was one handsome
country sheriff who hadn't gone to fat. He didn't
sound like a typical cracker either, the kind who sold
trucks on television commercials; his voice was soft,
rumbling, and warm, with a good-ole-boy chuckle just
waiting for an opportunity to surface. But there was a
warning in his eyes, which could go suddenly small,
shrewd, and piglike, and behind that chuckle was a
serpentine rattle. Buford Dodd was not a man to
cross.

"Reckon we wasted your time, coming all the way up here from Atlanta," Dodd said. Then he shook Beau's hand, hard. "But I been hearing about you the past couple of years, so I'm glad we had this opportunity to meet."

"Glad to meet you, too. Never a waste of time—just our job," Beau lied. "So, you've got the body here?" He glanced around the room, where three deputies slouched here and there like hunting dogs. The overhead fluorescent lights made everybody look dead.

"Yep."

"Had anybody look at it?"

"The coroner's been and gone. We're ready to release it to the family as soon as they get here."

"Who's the coroner in this county?"

"Doc Johnson." Dodd grinned slowly, sharing the joke with his deputies, who grinned back. "He's the vet."

Beau didn't even blink. "Mind if I take a look?"

Dodd hoisted his left buttock down off the counter where he'd been partially resting himself. "Not a'tall," he said, and led the way to the morgue.

Forrest Ridley had probably been a handsome man. But it was a little hard to tell after the vicious beating he'd taken—presumably down the almost 750 feet of rocky falls. Though the body was fully dressed, contusions and abrasions were apparent about the face; the nose and right arm and left leg were at angles that indicated fractures. The neck was broken. And the flesh showed that the body had been in the water for more than a couple of hours. It was fortunate that the weather had been cool.

Even so, the little room, whose walls were painted mint green, was filled with a distinctively sweet and nauseating odor.

"Guess they'll want to get him buried pretty quick," Dodd observed.

Beau raised an eyebrow, then nodded. "Guess so. Of course, they can do that since there'll be no autopsy. Do you mind?" He gestured toward the body.

"Be my guest."

Beau reached over and opened Forrest Ridley's mouth.

"What you looking for?" Dodd asked.

"Foam. You usually see it if the victim inhaled water while still alive."

"Huh." Three beats passed. "See any?"

"No."

"Well, I'd imagine he was already dead by the time he hit any considerable water, wouldn't you? Banging himself down all those drops from the top."

"Probably. What do you think caused *that?*" Beau was pointing at a round hole through the man's shirt just below the right shoulder, inches above the heart.

"Some of those rocks are awfully sharp. Fall like that, Doc Johnson said you're likely to see all kinds of things. Said you can't tell one thing from another."

"So, could you?" Samantha asked.

"Could I what?"

"Tell one thing from another?"

"I can tell you that what I was looking at was no puncture wound from a rock," Beau said, his face grim. "It was a gunshot exit if I ever saw one."

"So what are you going to do about it?"

"Nothing."

"Nothing? What do you mean, nothing?" Sam demanded.

"Samantha, you know as well as I do that Sheriff Dodd's judgment is law in his jurisdiction. If he says the man died accidentally, he did. Open and shut, no autopsy, no inquest. What I want to know is what *you're* going to do about it."

"Me?"

"I can't imagine that you're going to stop here, once you've got going. Not with a *body,* for Christ's sake."

"It's not my job. It's police business."

"Ha! Since when did that ever stop you?"

"How do *you* know what would stop me?"

He gave her a look. "I've read every word you ever wrote in the *Chronicle,* Sam. I know you don't get those kinds of stories by sitting on your sweet can waiting for the cops to feed you."

She ignored the anatomical reference, and she was *not* going to ask him why he'd read the San Francisco paper.

"Besides," he continued, "you're ignoring the fact that there's not going to *be* any investigation." He waved Bernice over and requested a fresh carafe of coffee. Then suddenly he grasped Sam's hand as she reached for the sugar. "Come on, Sam. Let's do this."

She jerked back as if the waitress had just scalded her. "What are you *talking* about?"

"I'm talking about working together on this story, this case, whatever you want to call it." His voice dropped. "I'm talking about spending some time with you."

Sam pushed her hands against the table, trying to get as much space between them as possible. She shook her head. She opened her mouth, but no words came.

He looked straight at her, unblinking, unwavering. "I made a terrible mistake when I let you go. I've paid for it ever since. I'm sorry. I've always been so terribly, terribly sorry."

She half-stood.

"Don't go."

"I don't want to talk about this." She held her hands in front of her as if to ward him off.

"Please. Just listen. I have so much I want to say to you. Every time I went to San Francisco, I'd hang out in front of your house for days, hoping to catch a glimpse of you. And since you've been back in Atlanta, I've visited my mother so much she's asked me if I want my old room back."

His old room that she could see from her bedroom window. The room she'd yelled curses at just the other night.

"I want to go back to that summer and do it all over," he said. "Do it differently this time, so we have a life together."

"What are you *talking* about? What about your wife?"

"Linda . . ." He shook his head, frowning. "It was a mistake, for both of us. Now she's met someone else. I always hoped she would. We've filed for a divorce."

"Well, that's great, that's just great!" Sam was out of the booth now. "I don't give a damn about you or your marriage. Do you understand that?" Heads turned. She was yelling. She couldn't stop herself.

"What makes you think I give a shit about how you feel, about me or anything else? You think you can just waltz back into my life after all these years? Are you crazy?"

"Probably."

"Well, you can take your crazy and shove it!" She headed for the door, picking up speed, out the door. She was wet. Shit! She'd left her umbrella. Forget it. She slammed the car door. Hard.

When she glanced over, he was standing outside her window in the pouring rain.

"You didn't hear a word I said," he yelled.

She looked up at his wet face. "I heard you, Beau." She rolled the window down just a crack. "I heard every word you said. But you said them about twenty years too late. What you think now has nothing to do with me. I don't owe you."

"I never said you did. I just want to spend time with you, Sam. I want to show you how sorry I am that I was such a creep."

She turned the key in the ignition. "Get away from my car."

"You going to run over me?"

"Maybe."

His voice dropped. "Do you hate me that much?"

"Maybe."

"They say hate's just the flip side of love."

She put the car in reverse, and he jumped back as it began to move. She called through the rain, "I wouldn't count on it."

She didn't even want to think about what Beau had said. It was too crazy. It'd make *her* crazy. She punched in a tape of Linda Ronstadt's greatest hits, turned up the volume, and sang along at the top of her lungs all the way home through the driving rain.

When she got there, George was in the study reading his mail with a magnifying glass. "Have you ever noticed that it's bills that come in the largest print?" he asked.

Samantha gave him a hug. He hugged her back. They made her feel safe—his hugs.

"Jehoshaphat, you're wet! What have you been up to this beautiful morning?"

George loved gray days. He said they gave him an excuse to do nothing but read.

Samantha threw herself into a chair facing her uncle and told him about her meeting with Beau, editing out the personal part, sharing with him what she'd learned about Ridley's death.

"What do you think he was doing up there in Watkin County, anyway?" she asked. "And I wonder how long he'd been there. How long has he been dead? Did he really go to San Francisco? Why? And why was Queen so funny about the trip? Who would want to kill Forrest Ridley?"

"Whoa. Wait a minute. Who said someone killed him? How do you know he didn't tumble over the falls, just like Dodd said?"

"I didn't say he didn't tumble. The words just popped out. But now that I've said them, I know that's it. It was murder, George."

He peered sharply at his niece, who had the same sixth sense, the same gift and curse, that he had always possessed. "You feel it?"

"In my bones."

He shifted in his chair, "Well, we'd better get busy."

He chewed on the earpiece of his glasses for a few moments, then said, "You know, Sam, when you got back to the *Constitution*'s morgue, you ought to do some looking into land up that way."

"Land? What does that have to do with the price of rice?"

"I don't know. Just a feeling."

They grinned at each other.

"But there's lots of money changing hands, big money, as the city pushes its way north," George continued. "There are some folks who commute from almost as far as Monroeville to work in Atlanta. Land values have gone through the roof up there."

"How about drugs? Didn't you say sometimes one can almost ski in those mountains on the white powder?"

George shook his head. "Could be. But I don't think so. I think land's what you ought to be studying. And I'll do some asking around."

"How do you know Forrest Ridley wasn't just doing a little fishing and was robbed and killed?"

"Man didn't fish."

"Camping?"

"Not the type."

"Hiking?" Sam asked. "I know he went for long walks. Their housekeeper said so."

"Could be."

"But you don't think so?"

"No, I don't."

"Then what *do* you think?"

"I think the whole thing's odd, that's what I think. I think Forrest Ridley was the kind of man who, except for walking his dog, thought of exercise as the reach between his office door and that of a limo or taxi. I think he mostly spent his time working and making money, unless . . ."

"Unless what?"

"Well, Liza told you he wasn't really happy with Queen."

"So?"

"So *cherchez la femme,* my dear."

"You're a dirty old man, George."

"Never said I wasn't."

Seven

$\blacklozenge$

"YOU'RE DOING WHAT?"

"Hoke, you're shouting. I'm not deaf." Samantha held the phone away from her ear.

"No, but you sure as hell must be dumb. What do you mean, you're working on the Forrest Ridley story? There *is* no Forrest Ridley story. We have an obit writer, thank you. And a fine job she does, for an old lady who should have retired ten years ago."

"I think someone murdered him, Hoke."

"The police say it was an accidental death, case closed. But *you* know better?"

"Sheriff Dodd of Watkin County declared it an accidental death. That's not the same thing."

The line was silent except for the sound of Hoke's sucking on a cigarette—and then he was shouting again. "You'd do *anything* for this corrupt sheriff thing, wouldn't you? Even if you have to make it up. It's not Forrest Ridley you're interested in. It's the sheriff!"

Sam stared at the receiver in her hand for a minute. It *was* an interesting coincidence—but no more than a coincidence. "I feel it in my bones, Hoke. There's something there. You're going to be sorry if we miss this one."

"With the power Simmons and Lee wields in this town, I'm not so sure if this is going to be good news or bad news. Providing, of course, that you aren't just whistling Dixie."

Sam smiled. She'd hooked him. "Why, Hoke, I don't know what you mean. I'm not even sure I remember the tune." And then she hung up the phone—which rang again immediately. "Hello?"

"Sam?"

"Liza? Dear, I'm so sorry about your—"

"Can you meet me at Manuel's? Now, please? It's very important."

The bar was fairly empty on this rainy afternoon. Remembering that she hadn't yet had lunch, Sam settled herself into a booth facing the back door and ordered a dozen oysters on the half shell and a Virgin Mary.

Manuel's Tavern on North Highland was, like the Varsity, an Atlanta institution. The original barroom with booths along one side was decorated with execrable paintings of proprietor Manuel Maloof's heroes, FDR and JFK, as well as some pretty awful nudes. Long a favorite hangout of the city's journalists and drinking liberals, it was a loud, comfortable, masculine watering hole. However, women were not only welcome, but protected by the ever-watchful bartenders. It hadn't changed a whit in more than two decades. Sam hoped it never would.

"Hi, Sam. How's George?" Manuel called from the bar. No matter how long a regular was away, Manuel always remembered, even though he had become a power in DeKalb County politics and had other things on his mind.

"Fine. He doesn't get out as much these days. I'll have to drag him in soon."

"You do that. Awful about Forrest Ridley, isn't it? I remember a party he gave once in one of the back rooms. It was . . ." Manuel's words trailed off as he recognized the dead man's daughter coming through the back door.

Samantha rose. "Over here, Liza."

The girl's eyes were hidden behind dark glasses, which completed her all-black costume. She was dressed much the same as the last time Sam had seen her—could that have been only yesterday? But today her black garb wasn't a punk artist's affectation. Today it was mourning.

"I'm so sorry," Sam began as she had on the telephone, and again got no further as Liza waved her sympathy away. The girl couldn't talk about that now—the fact that her father was dead, that she was never going to see him again, never going to place another basketball bet, never going to hear him call her by his pet name, "Miss." She could only deal with the tangential.

"She's locked herself in her room," Liza said. Sam didn't have to ask to know she was talking about Queen. "She's hardly said a word to me—as if *she* were the only one . . ." Her voice broke. She took a deep breath and regrouped. "She's constantly on the phone."

"To whom?"

"I don't know. She has a private line. But"—Liza removed her dark glasses and stared straight at Sam—"I listened at the door once. She was saying, 'Well, we don't have long to wait, not anymore.'"

"What do you think that meant?"

"What do *you* think?"

Sam was tempted to say *I asked you first,* but refrained. "I don't know. She could be talking about anything. What do you *really* think, Liza?"

"I think someone killed my father."

The girl's bluntness took Sam's breath away. "Why do you think that?"

"He's—he *was*—not a stupid man. He's not going to go fooling around up there at the top of Apalachee and just *fall.* It's clearly marked."

"You're sure?"

"Of course. the falls aren't all that far from Tate, where we've always spent at least part of every summer."

"Your family?"

"All of us. The partners and their families. We're all one big happy family, don't you know?"

"You don't really mean that."

Liza gestured with one hand. "We *used* to be. When I was a little girl, I loved to go up to Tate. But when I was about fourteen, it started to change. Or *I* started to change. It began to choke me."

"Tate did?"

"The whole thing. You don't know what it's like."

"Try me."

"Well, maybe you do." Liza sighed. "Everyone's the same. There are rules for everything. What you do. What you say. Who you see. Where you go to school. What you wear, eat, think—or *don't* think.

100

Everyone follows the party line, the S and L party line."

"And that's so bad?"

"It's all about money, and walking the acceptable straight and narrow, and being *us*, which is the same as being right. Whatever they are is *right*. Do you understand what I mean?"

"Yes," Sam said softly. It was very familiar. She'd stood in Liza's shoes many years before.

"I'm a painter," Liza said. "I couldn't *do* all that."

"And your father didn't force you?"

"You know, sometimes I used to think that he saw a part of himself in me. A part that wanted to stand up in a partners' meeting and say, 'Fuck you.'"

"Would he ever have done that?"

"No." Liza shook her head. "Not really. He'd bought too far into the system for too long. He wouldn't have had anything left afterwards. He wouldn't have known what to do after the big silence, after he'd walked out the door."

Sam marveled at this young girl. She herself hadn't been half as smart at her age. Not *this* kind of smart, anyway.

"Who would have wanted to hurt your father, Liza?"

She shook her head again. "I don't know. I've been thinking about that since I heard . . . I've been thinking and, well, after Queen . . ."

"You *really* suspect your mother?"

"I wouldn't trust her as far as I could throw her. She's not a nice woman, Sam. She only cares about one person in the whole world—Queen. She thinks she *is*, you know, a queen."

"Funny, her name."

"She earned it."

"What do you mean?"

"She wasn't *christened* that. Her real name is Catherine. But she was so taken with herself, even as a child, that her mammy nicknamed her that, and it stuck. I've heard her tell that on herself—in one of her rare fine moods."

"But you're implying that she killed your father. That's a far cry from self-importance," Sam pointed out. "Why would she want to do that?"

"Maybe he'd changed his mind about leaving her." Liza played with a strand of her dark hair. "I don't know. But they'd been having some awful fights lately."

"Anyone else you suspect?" Sam signaled the waiter to bring another beer for Liza.

"It's probably nothing . . ."

"Nothing's nothing. Tell me."

"Well, Daddy did a lot of *pro bono* work. I don't think any of the other partners ever did." Then she smiled. "Except he said your uncle used to."

"Still does." Sam nodded.

"Anyway, Daddy always said that besides helping some poor bastard out of a jam, he liked to keep his hand in everyday trial work. His practice was much more esoteric than that."

"What did he do?"

"Bonds. I never understood any of it, except that it all had to do with corporations and tons of money."

"Go on," Sam prodded.

"Well, about six months ago, he took the case of one of the Mariels in the Atlanta federal pen."

"Explain."

"You know, the prisoners Castro freed from that awful prison? When they came here, the government put most of them right back in jail, until the political prisoners could be sorted out from the murderers. Anyway, this woman, Maria Ortega, had heard about Daddy's work and begged him to take on her father's case. She said her father, Carlos, was a good man who had already served fifteen years for nothing. So Daddy pled his case, and he won."

"And?"

"And within a month after being released, Carlos Ortega killed a grocery store owner's wife in an armed robbery. The man who owned the store, Herman Blanding, blamed Daddy. At the second trial, which Daddy attended every day because he felt so awful, so responsible, Mr. Blanding stood up when Ortega was convicted and said that it was all Daddy's fault, that if he hadn't gotten Ortega out of jail, his wife would still be alive. He came to Daddy's office a couple of weeks later and said he was going to get him."

"Did your dad call the police?" Sam asked.

"No. He sort of shrugged it off. Not the whole affair, I mean, he lost sleep over *that*, agonized over it. But not the threat. Queen said he ought to start carrying a gun, but he wouldn't. He hated guns."

"Really?"

"His younger brother was killed when he was very young. In a hunting accident. Daddy never touched a gun after that."

Samantha wanted to ask what Forrest Ridley's role had been in that accident, but she couldn't bring herself to form the words. You're getting soft, she thought. There was a time, Samantha . . . Yes, there had been times when she'd asked questions that were sharp as knives while the scent of blood was still fresh in the air. Maybe she *hadn't* been kidding when she told George she wasn't doing murders anymore. So what was she doing here? Doing things half-assed, that's what. Well, hell. Maybe the question wasn't important. Quit jacking yourself around, Sam, she told herself. To a good journalist, *all* questions, *all* answers, are important.

But she skipped it and went on. "What do you know about your parents' 'surprise' party?"

Liza managed a laugh. "You mean the one that was such a surprise to Queen?"

"Your father, too, I thought."

"Yeah, but stuff like that rolls—rolled—off his back like water. But Queen"—she laughed again—"Queen was livid. Whoever came up with that one, it worked. She was in such a fit, I thought she was going to make another trip to her plastic surgeon."

"Her what?"

"Queen is a major supporter of Dr. Tuckit in Rio."

"Are you kidding?"

"No. Well, yes, I'm kidding about his name. Queen has had everything that can be lifted and tucked or pooched out"—Liza gestured at her own modest chest—"till she's like a bionic woman. When she gets the slightest bit depressed, she flies down to Rio and has something reworked."

Well, no *wonder* she looked so good. "The party," Sam said. "Did she ever find out who did it?" She remembered then that Horace was going to work on that, but things had happened so quickly that she hadn't thought to ask him.

"No. I don't think so. But there *was* one thing more." Liza looked Sam straight in the eyes again. There was something about the girl's candor that was almost alarming. "The next day, after the party, a note arrived in the mail."

"Did you see it?"

"Yes. Daddy showed it to me."

"Handwritten?"

Liza made a face. "Don't be silly. Typed. It said, 'Do you'—no, '*Did* you like your surprise? There'll be more you'll like even less.'"

"Were there?"

"More surprises? No. Not that I know of." And then, as the possibility of what that surprise might have been crossed her mind, it was reflected in her blue eyes. "Unless Daddy's . . ."

Sam reached for the girl's hand. "We'll find out."

Back home, Sam found George in his study. "Liza thinks he was murdered, too."

"You think what we have is catching?"

Sam shrugged. "No one else agrees with us. I just put in a call to Charlie downtown."

"What'd he say?"

"Far as he knows, it's an open-and-shutter. Said the department wasn't going out of its way looking for trouble."

"Fine attitude for the police," sniffed Peaches, who was passing the room.

"How do you know who Charlie is?" Sam asked, startled. Even Hoke didn't know the name of her contact in the police department.

"God didn't give people ears to be used as jug

handles," Peaches replied. "Do you think I've lived in this house all these years and don't know the price of beans?"

"So much for that, mixed-metaphorically speaking," George said, grinning.

"I reckon." Sam grinned back.

Eight

◆

"RIDLEY WOULD HAVE BEEN PROUD," GEORGE SAID as he and Sam stood on the steps of St. Philip's Cathedral watching the huge crowd pour out into the spring sunshine. Everyone who was anyone in town had come to pay their last respects. "You couldn't have asked for a more beautiful day for a funeral."

"I thought beautiful days were for weddings, not funerals," Sam said.

"No, no. You don't want everyone thinking their last thoughts of you on a dreary day, or in the pouring rain. Course, if I had my druthers, I don't think I'd have gone out the way Ridley did."

"Nor would anyone, I imagine." Sam shivered at the thought of all that water, those rocks, the horror Ridley must have felt as he tipped over the edge and realized he was going for the big fall—if he was alive when he went over.

"I don't mean the mu—" George broke off and lowered his voice. "The murder. But when I go, I'd like for it to be prolonged, drawn out."

"You can't mean that!"

"I do. It'd be like my eyesight going slowly—it's not such a shock. I have time to look at all the things I love, to memorize them, in a way to say good-bye. I'd like to leave this coil that way, too. With time to say 'I love you,' to set things right."

Sam thought about her uncle's words, and then about her beloved Sean, who was there one evening, his sweet face in her hands, the next morning not. She stared off into space, down the steps and across a sea of dark suits and ladies' navy straw hats, then started as she realized she was looking straight into Beau Talbot's eyes. He looked away and finished tucking Liza Ridley into the long black limousine by which he was standing. In the midst of Edison Kay's eulogy of her father, Liza had finally collapsed. Beau, sitting a couple of rows behind the Ridley family, had come forward and taken her out a side door. Now Liza was as pale as the dogwood blossoms in the churchyard, but seemed composed. Beau's face was somber. He looked back up at Sam and nodded.

"Well done," George said, shaking the hand of Edison Kay.

"Terrible thing. Terrible. I've known Forrest as an associate and a friend for thirty years. We started as puppies together."

"I remember." George smiled a little. "Neither of you knew a tort from a tart."

"Hell, you're right about that," Edison said with a chuckle. "And you taught us the difference, didn't you, old man?" He ducked his head toward Samantha. "'Scuse us old dogs."

Sam was about to reply when Edison suddenly erupted, "What's that son-of-a-bitch doing here?"

He was staring at a tall, gangly, gray-haired man in a scruffy old ankle-length gray coat. The man's complexion was ashen too—he was a monochrome study.

"Who you talking about?" George's head turned in the right direction, but he couldn't see that far.

"Herman Blanding. That bastard who came into the office threatening Forrest's life, blamed him for his wife's death. Hell, I warned Forrest he ought not to mess around with those *pro bono* cases, with spics, white trash. See how much gratitude you get. Bastards like that!" Edison's voice was loud. Heads turned.

So *that* was Herman Blanding. Sam started toward him. The gray man looked past her, his weak, pink-rimmed eyes staring into Edison Kay's face; then he turned and shuffled away, disappearing into the crush.

Shortly after the burial service in Oakwood Cemetery, some of that same well-dressed crush was drinking bourbon and dunking shrimp in cocktail sauce in Queen Ridley's all-white living room.

"In the old days, we'd have all sent over baked hams and covered dishes," said one of the wives Sam recognized from the Kays' party.

"Leave it to Queen to have a wake catered. Well, she might as well. It'll be *her* last big do for a while."

"Why, Kay Kay, you should be ashamed!"

Sam turned. Yes, it was Kay Kay who would win today's Nine Lives competition.

The former Texas beauty queen continued sharpening her claws. "She'll have to lie low for a while, maybe make another trip to Rio before she comes hunting. You better hold on to Clifford, old girl," she said to a woman with blued hair standing beside her.

"I reckon it's going to be the *big* bucks she's gonna come after. I'm not letting Edison out of the house till Queen's bagged her a man and tied him to the bedpost."

The women clucked, but their eyes encouraged Kay Kay as she warmed up.

"I been thinking about getting my *whole body* snatched up from the top of my head," Kay Kay continued. "Just pull it all up from my toes. It's what you got to do, girls, if you want to keep up with the competition."

Were *all* unattached women the competition? Sam wondered, snagging a glass of soda from a passing waiter. Was *she* the competition? Of course she was—which was why she never got invitations from this crowd, not that she cared. You couldn't take a chance on an extra woman in the game of marital musical chairs.

"God, you're beautiful in black."

She didn't even turn her head. She would recognize that voice until the day she died.

She'd thought about him last night after she'd gone to bed—when she couldn't avoid the thoughts any longer.

There had been a time, oh, there'd been a *long* time when she would have given anything in the world to hear Beau say the things he'd said to her yesterday.

But now? Now she was grown-up. That's what she'd decided last night. He'd been only a young girl's crush—a summer romance, her first lover. The choice of immature judgment. But there'd been nothing *substantial* between them.

What about the lust?

So what about it?

110

So *what* about it?

She lusted after lots of people: Mel Gibson, Sam Shepard, Jeff Bridges. That didn't mean she'd take off her clothes and lie down in the street for them.

Well, maybe—if they weren't movie stars, if she really knew them.

She knew Beau.

Which was probably why, when she heard his voice, despite her best intentions the little hairs stood up on the back of her neck.

"Don't call me beautiful," she hissed.

"I didn't. I said you were beautiful in black. There's a difference. But you *are* beautiful."

She tried to move away, but the crowd was too close. Sam turned back to face him. Then the mob shifted and pushed her bosom into his chest. She glared up at him.

"I'm not saying a word." He grinned.

"You'd better not. How's Liza?"

Beau's face sobered. "I put her to bed upstairs with a sedative. She ought to sleep for at least twelve hours. She's all in." He paused and took a deep breath, which she shared, of course. "So, what do you think, Sam?"

"What do I think about what?"

"About our working on this together."

"No."

"Why not?"

She rolled her eyes.

"Verbalize, please," he said.

"Because I don't want to work with you."

"So you agree there is something to work *on.*"

She shrugged, which, given their proximity, wasn't such a good idea.

"Who've you talked to?" he continued.

"Nobody. Well, Uncle George."

"And?"

"Hoke, who thinks I'm nuts."

"Well, Hoke is either very off or very on."

Sam remembered that the two men were childhood friends.

"Yes, and?" he pressed.

"Liza."

"What'd she say?"

"That she thinks someone . . ." Then Sam realized she couldn't go on, not with so many ears so close. She shook her head.

"See," Beau whispered, leaning down, "we need to get together and talk."

"We *are* together and talking."

He ignored that. "Have you spoken with Queen again?"

"No."

"Are you going to?"

She'd been thinking about that. She had lots of questions for the Widow Ridley. But how was she going to approach her? She couldn't just call. This was a house of mourning. She looked into Beau's eyes as she slipped the pearl and diamond earring from her right ear.

"What are you going to do with that?"

"Leave it," she whispered.

"Where?"

"Under there." She pointed to a chair.

Beau smiled. "When?"

"When the crowd moves."

"Moves where?"

"What do you—" Then she looked around. The

crowd *had* moved, but she hadn't. And of course, he'd let her keep standing there, pressed breast to chest.

She flung her earring under the chair and sashayed out of the room without a backward glance. She knew the smirk on his face. She didn't need to look.

Back home, Harpo met her at the door holding his mouth crooked. The next step, she knew, would be his fake limp.

"Don't try to make me feel guilty, dog," she told him. "I've been hard at a funeral."

"He wants a bath," Peaches said. "When I came home from my meeting at the mayor's office, he was standing in George's bathroom staring at the tub."

"Why do I have a dog who's a clean freak?"

"You might get in there yourself and take a long soak. It would relax you some."

"Don't I look relaxed?"

"No. You look like twenty miles of bad road," Peaches said flatly.

"Thanks."

"I'm just telling you what I see. Who'd *you* see today? You see the murderer at Forrest Ridley's funeral?"

Sam started to answer *What murderer?* but she knew Peaches knew better. Peaches knew *everything*.

"I might have," she said. "I don't know."

Upstairs, she gave Harpo a quick shampoo and wrapped him in a towel, then rinsed the tub, filled it with hot water and bath oil, and stepped in. After a quarter of an hour, she reached for the phone.

"What's up, Cookieface?" answered Cutting, her best tracker in San Francisco. "Where are you?"

"In the tub."

"God," he sighed. "It's times like this I wish I weren't fifty-nine, fat, and gray."

"We can still talk dirty."

"Please, my heart can't stand it."

Then Cutting listened carefully to what she wanted.

"If Ridley was in a hotel in this town recently, I'll get it for you, and the names of any roommates," he promised. "Now, get out of there before you pucker."

The call to the local Drug Enforcement Administration office was business all the way. Yes, her contact said, Buford Dodd was a suspect in drug drops in Watkin County. But so were lots of other folks.

"These country boys can be mean," the agent warned. "And I apologize for sounding like a chauvinist oink when I say this, Ms. Adams, but it's no business for a lady. I wouldn't sniff around these boys if I was you, even if I knew I had the right tree. They hurt you real bad when they fall."

Nine

◆

WHAT *EXACTLY* IS IT THAT YOU WANT TO KNOW, Samantha?" Queen Ridley rose, stiff-backed, from her white sofa. "What are all these questions about that unfortunate 'surprise' party leading toward?" She lit a cigarette and exhaled through her lovely nose. "Or is this just some peculiar brand of torture that you reporters reserve for the bereaved?"

"Queen, I . . ." Blew it. Came on too fast, too strong.

"You *are* here as press, aren't you? Asking questions about my—*our* personal lives. Isn't that why you left your earring behind?"

Sam's years of training stood her in good stead. She didn't miss a beat. "No, truly, that was an accident. And I'm terribly sorry if I've offended you."

Queen stood with her head bowed just a tad. It was quite some pose, the mourning Queen, sad but imperious, perfectly coiffed and made up. Shiny as ever, the Widow Ridley was in gray silk. Had Sam caught her on her way out to a dinner party?

"Thank you for coming by," Queen was saying now as if she had just ended an audience. She paused at the bottom of the stairs. "I'm very tired. If you'll excuse me." She even managed a break in her voice on those last words, and then she floated upward.

Sam stood there debating. Did she dare slip into the kitchen to say hello to Lona? Or upstairs to see Liza? Too risky. Queen could come back down at any second. She turned and opened the front door.

Suddenly Oglethorpe raced past her like a black and white cannonball.

Lona was right behind him. "Ogle! You bad dog!"

Sam joined the chase down the front steps and across the lawn. The two of them charged along the sidewalk after the galloping dog. They caught up with him a block from Piedmont Park.

"Oh, thank you," Lona gasped when she had the Dalmatian, whose tongue was lolling in a silly grin, firmly by the collar.

Then they turned and started back toward the house. Lona shook her head. Her imaginary silver bangles clanged silently. "I don't know *what* I'm going to do with him now, with Mr. Ridley . . ." She trailed off, her lip trembling.

So Lona had liked Forrest Ridley. Well, why wouldn't she? As far as Sam knew, everyone had—except Herman Blanding. She made a mental note to see Blanding as soon as possible.

"I heard what you asked Miz Queen about that surprise party," Lona said. "Did she tell you about the note that came afterwards?"

Sam shook her head. No, she hadn't—Liza had.

"They talked about it at the breakfast table," Lona went on. "Miz Queen sure had a bee in her bonnet."

"And Ridley?"

"He took it in stride, like he did everything else. He just laughed." Her face clouded over then. "What do you think really happened up there?"

"I think he fell over Apalachee Falls. What do you think?"

"I think he was too smart to do anything foolish like that. I think somebody pushed him."

"Who?" Sam asked bluntly.

Lona shook her head, but her face said she had her suspicions.

Two young neighborhood boys yelled greetings at Oglethorpe as they wheeled past on their bicycles. The dog lunged against Lona's grip, but she was stronger than she looked. He was going nowhere.

"Now who's gonna walk this monster all the way across the park every night?"

"Is that where Ridley took him?"

"I never was sure. They took off in this direction most nights. Right after supper, just as I'd be heading out. I don't know exactly where they went."

"Or for how long?"

"Nope. As I said, it was always when I was going. But Miz Queen used to say . . ." She paused.

Sam waited. She knew Lona didn't need urging. She'd gotten onto the woman's rhythm by now. The delays were caused by her thoughtfulness; she was weighing and measuring.

"Miz Queen used to be after Mr. Ridley all the time. Said he spent a lot more time with that dog than he did with her."

"Was that true?"

"Just the two of them?" She nodded. "That's for sure. But then"—a smile pulled at the corners of her mouth—"Ogle didn't give him any backtalk."

"You know what I'd like to know, Lona? I'd really like to know where Mr. Ridley went every night with this dog. Do you think if you gave him his head, he'd go on that same walk?"

"Looks like it to me. Every chance he gets, he heads out in this direction."

"Not now, because I think Queen might wonder," Sam said. "But some other time . . ."

Lona nodded. "I'll see where he wants to go. And I'll get you that party note. You'll find out what happened to Mr. Ridley."

It was a statement, not a question. Sam wished she felt that confident.

"Will he know what this is in reference to?" asked the secretary in one of those officious voices that made Sam want to fire off a smart answer. But the woman held the keys to the kingdom, so Sam held her tongue.

"Yes, he will," she nicey-niced into the phone.

But of course he wouldn't. Edison Kay would have no idea why Samantha was calling him, but he wouldn't care, either—he found her an attractive woman. Sam knew that. Years ago as a cub reporter, she had inspected her arsenal and evaluated all its weapons.

"Why, Samantha dear, to what do I owe this pleasure? No, don't tell me now. Why don't you tell me over lunch?"

"Why, that's awfully sweet of you," she crooned,

standing off to one side in her mind and listening to how well she dropped into her Southern belle voice these days. "But I'm afraid I have a previous engagement. What I called for, Edison, is to make an appointment with you for some other time."

"I'm at your disposal."

"Actually, I'd like to talk to both you and Kay Kay—and Totsie. We've decided to do a longer piece on Forrest Ridley for the Sunday magazine, a profile, and I'd like to have the input of those who knew him best."

She knew that Edison wouldn't know that that was not the sort of thing she did—nor did the *Constitution* know about any such story. The whole thing was a fabrication.

She really wanted to know more about Ridley and his practice and what skeletons might therein lie, and who better to ask than oily Edison, who was not only Ridley's partner but such a good friend that he had delivered his eulogy? She was also curious about Kay Kay, who had bad-mouthed the deceased's wife at his wake. And Totsie . . . There was more to Totsie than met the eye, and she'd known Ridley since the day she was born.

"Why, that's a wonderful idea. I'll have to check with Kay Kay's calendar. That woman's busier than I am." He chuckled. There was a pause while he stuck a cigar in his mouth; Sam could hear him sucking on it. "Now, you're sure you won't change your mind about joining me for lunch?"

"Peaches, you have outdone yourself again," George said, pushing back from the dinner table later that evening. She'd made crab cakes, pencil-thin asparagus, a green salad. For dessert there'd been the first of the season's strawberries over her shortcake.

"Glad you liked it," Peaches said, smiling. Though she could be vinegary, she was all honey when someone praised her cooking.

"One of these days I'm going to have to get my friend Annie to write one of her food articles on you," said Sam. "You're a walking cookbook just waiting for the doing."

"Don't say that," George protested. "We see her little enough as it is. I couldn't bear for Peaches to become a star."

"Get out of here," Peaches said, but she was still smiling. "Scat, both of you. I've got work to do."

"Why don't we take our coffee out on the front porch?" Sam suggested.

"A capital idea," said George.

The porch was actually a terrace, a stone-floored continuation of the front entrance, which no one ever used. They settled into black wrought-iron chairs sporting a patina of green.

"*Now* I remember why we never sit out here," George grumbled. "Horace," he said as the man approached with a tray loaded with the small silver after-dinner coffeepot and George's cognac. "Tomorrow I want all this furniture to go to the Lighthouse for the Blind's resale shop. And I want you to find me some wicker chairs with soft cushions and a good-sized table to match."

"They won't hold up." Horace was ever practical about George's money.

"I don't give a damn. If they rot, we'll get new ones next year, and every year after that. I am not going to spend my old age with this goddamned uncomfortable furniture stamping its imprint into my butt."

"Yes, George," Horace said. "I'll call Rich's tomorrow." Then, just as he was about to turn away, he slipped an envelope in front of Samantha as if it were an afterthought.

He should have been an actor, Sam thought as she slit the envelope. His timing was perfect.

Inside were two sheets of paper. One was the folded and refolded note to the Ridleys that had arrived after the surprise party.

Liza was right. It was typewritten, with no errors, no erasures. And her quote was exact: *Did you like your surprise? There'll be more you'll like even less.* The words practically jumped off the plain white paper.

Samantha shivered.

"What is it?" George asked.

She handed him the note, and inspected the second sheet, smaller, lined, and inscribed with pencil. But she began to wave it as if it were an engraved invitation from the Princess of Wales.

"This is it! Listen: '202 Virginia Circle is where Oglethorpe goes. Lona.'"

"Huzzah!" cried George.

"Can I get you anything else?" asked Horace.

"Tell me something," Sam said. "How'd you do that so fast? I saw Lona only this morning."

"Telegraph's built for speed," he replied enigmatically and then turned to leave.

"Beats the hell out of computers, doesn't it?" asked George.

"Now, a computer is just a bunch of zeros," Horace responded, changing his mind about his exit.

"I went and looked at one the last time I was in Rich's. It was cold. I like dealing with people myself. They can be in a real hurry, if they see that it's something you need—and something they care about with their hearts. As far as I can see, a computer doesn't care about anything."

Peaches appeared at the front door. "Dr. Talbot's on the phone for you, Sam," she announced, her voice as cool and noncommittal as if Beau, who hadn't rung this house that she knew of in almost two decades, did so every day.

As Samantha left the porch, Peaches asked, "So what have you all been talking about? Did I hear computers? I suppose you two old men are thinking about joining the bandwagon of high tech?"

"I knew it was going to come to this," Horace said to George, "when they gave her that first computer down at the literacy program office."

"Well, I told you then that there are four-year-old children those machines have taught to read," Peaches retorted.

"Does that mean you think we're dumber than four-year-olds if we don't get one?" George asked.

"I just said then, and I'll repeat, there's illiterate and there's illiterate, if you know what I mean."

"Horace, would you please buy Peaches a computer while you're at Rich's getting the wicker furniture? We might as well, because there's uncomfortable and there's uncomfortable, if you know what I mean."

"I do," Horace said, "I do indeed know what you mean."

Sam took the call in the kitchen.
"So?" Beau said.

"So what?"

"So what happened when you went to see Queen?"

Sam held the receiver out in front of her for a moment and stared at it.

"How are we going to work together on this case if you don't keep me up on the skinny?" Beau complained.

"There's a real obvious answer, Beau. We aren't."

He was unflappable. "So what do you think? Did she kill him for his money? Or because he was stepping out on her?"

"What makes you think that?"

"Which?"

"That there was another woman?"

"Often is, isn't there?"

There was a long pause before Sam said, "Yes, Beau. Quite frequently, yes."

He cleared his throat. "Well, did she give *anything* away?"

Sam looked down at Lona's envelope, which she was still holding. "Can you take fingerprints off paper?"

"Sure, if we're lucky."

She told him about the surprise party note.

"It's probably been handled to hell and gone. Am I right?"

"Right. Me, George, Lona, Liza, Queen, Ridley, God knows who else."

"Well, it's worth a try anyway. But you're going to have to get me smooth prints of everyone you just named."

"Mine are on file at the paper."

"And Ridley's I can get from the—hell, no," he said, "I can't. There *was* no autopsy."

"But he was an attorney."

"You're right. He's on file with the PD. What about the others? Can you manage them?"

Sam thought about how quickly Lona had worked through Horace earlier in the day. "I think so."

Beau's voice was excited. "Now we're cooking. The physical evidence never lies. That's why I love it. Your hunches and my facts—we're gonna be a great team, Ms. Adams."

"We are *not*."

"You want to be a glory hog? No problem. You don't have to give me a word of credit. Just helping you is enough. I'll be plenty satisfied."

"Oh, Lord." What was happening here? It was like a seduction: she kept saying no and he kept going right ahead.

"Send the prints right over when you get them. Or I can pick them up when I get home."

"What?"

"When I get home tonight. Didn't I tell you we've filed for a divorce? I moved into Mother's house yesterday. I'll be right across the street."

"You *what?*"

And with that bit of news, he rang off.

Ten

THE NEXT MORNING SAM WAS HEADED TOWARD THE Virginia Circle address Lona had given her when she came upon a crash between a fire engine and a garbage truck. A motorcycle cop waved her in precisely the opposite direction from where she wanted to go. She was driving south toward Grant Park, Oakland Cemetery, and Cabbagetown, looking for a place to turn around, when it dawned on her—Cabbagetown! Veering from the right turn she'd been about to make, she winced at the screech of brakes behind her. Herman Blanding, the all-gray man who'd threatened Forrest Ridley's life, lived in Cabbagetown. He was second on her list; she'd move him up one.

Cabbagetown was a residential community that grew up around the skirts of the Fulton Bag and Cotton Mill in the nineteenth century. It initially housed employees of the factory, who at the century's turn numbered some 700 souls transforming bales of Georgia cotton into finished cloth. As World War II created a demand for sandbags for bunkers and bomb shelters, Fulton Bag grew more prosperous, hiring almost 3,000 workers working in three shifts around the clock. Smokestacks rising from the red brick buildings spewed exhaust across the neighborhood; the reverberating looms shook the small shotgun houses. Charles Dickens would have felt at home in Cabbagetown when Fulton Bag was at its height.

The mill was shuttered now, absorbed into first one conglomerate and then another, and finally closed because its old-fashioned methodology, working from raw material to finished product, made it noncompetitive. But the neighborhood remained, its small one- and two-family tin-roofed frame houses threatened by yet another modern specter, gentrification, as young people seeking close-in, affordable places to live moved in.

"We shall not be moved" was the motto of the residents, holding on in their poor little houses on winding, sometimes unpaved streets. These were descendants of the rural Georgians who'd come from the mountains and the plains to find employment in the big city. "Recalcitrant white trash" was what the real estate speculators called them. "Proud" was what they called themselves as they planted signs reading "Speculators Keep Out" amidst the cabbage roses.

There was a sign, too, on the front porch of Herman Blanding's house on Pearl Street. The "KEEP OUT!" was printed. Scrawled in a slanting hand below were the words "This means YOU!!"

Any reporter worth her salt ignored such warnings. As she approached the tumbledown, peeling house, Sam cocked her head to the left to correct its fifteen-degree list. On the front porch was piled an amazing collection of goods, the sort often seen around houses in the country. But one rarely found such a hodge-podge of old sewing machines, car parts, furniture, tires, wooden crates, and broken bottles within city limits. Sam picked her way through the littered yard for a better look.

As her foot touched the bottom step, a fiend of hell lunged out of the moldering debris and, with its loud bark and hot breath, nearly took her head off.

She stumbled backwards as if in slow motion, fearing that this long, loud second was her last, aware of her thundering heartbeat, forgetting to take a breath. Then out of the maelstrom, she heard a man call: "Who is it, General Lee? Did you kill 'em yet?"

The torn screen door screeched open on its one remaining hinge, and the all-gray man she had seen at Ridley's funeral stepped out into a tiny clear space on the front porch. He patted the raging German shepherd, who instantly calmed at his touch. Herman Blanding was monochromatic again today, but this time his garb was no overcoat. He was decked out, cap to boots, in the frayed uniform of an officer of the Confederate States of America.

"General Lee will tear your throat out if you come any closer," he said in a voice that sounded as if it, like the door, could use oiling. He peered at her with squinting, weak eyes, his hand resting on his sword hilt. His gray hair was like rotten straw peeking out from the edges of his cap.

There was a clanking, and Sam noticed with relief that the dog was on a heavy chain. Of course, Blanding could loose him, but she began to breathe again.

I'm going to stand here and talk to this man, she thought. God, I'm brave. God, I'm terrified.

"Good day, Mr. Blanding."

"How do you know my name?" he shrilled. "They've been spying on me again!"

"I'm Samantha Adams. I'm here to talk with you about—" But she never finished the sentence.

"Stone Mountain!" Blanding cried, naming the huge granite outcropping near town. "Why . . . Stonewall, and Lee, and Jeff Davis! It's a pity, a travesty, I tell you, their faces having to look down at all that harlotry. Skating rinks! Riverboats! They've built a goddamned amusement park right there at their feet."

They don't have feet, she wanted to say. The carvings of the three Confederate generals, like those on Mount Rushmore, were of heads only. But she didn't think Blanding wanted to hear that.

"Why, did I think, when I was up on that hill"—he pointed in the direction of Oakland Cemetery, which was just on the other side of the defunct factory—"looking down on the Union troops advancing in the Battle of Atlanta, did I think to myself: General Hood, this rolling mill"—he pointed at Fulton Bag—"this rolling mill is going to make great condominiums one day? Hell, no, missy! I didn't! I thought: We've got to save the mill or we won't have any armor." He pointed in a different direction. "We've got to save the railroad, or we won't have reinforcements from Decatur. We've got to stop the Yankees in their tracks! That's what I thought. I didn't think about any goddamned condominiums!"

"No, sir." She nodded.

Blanding focused on her as if he hadn't known she was there until that second. "What's your name, miss? Would you like to come in and set for a spell, have a glass of iced tea? I don't get many visitors. It'd make me proud if you could."

Sure, General Hood, Sam thought. Yes sirree bob. Never had tea with a Confederate general before.

Sam slid through the screen door that Blanding was holding open for her. General Lee followed, sniffing the hem of her denim skirt. Blanding/Hood brought up the rear.

The front room in which she found herself was as cluttered as the front porch, but this jumble was thematic. The room was a memorial to Susan Blanding, Herman's wife. Photographs of her, from infancy to late middle age, created a bizarre wallpaper. Her clothes, shoes, stockings, and underwear were flung in little heaps, much as a woman might leave in her boudoir in a flurry of dressing or undressing. Bottles of her perfume were open on a mirrored tray, filling the air with the sweet smell of Shalimar. A small table, which was almost covered with her books and letters, was set for two.

"Were you expecting someone?" Sam asked Blanding, who had disappeared through a curtained door into what she assumed was the kitchen.

"Why, yes, Susan. You."

Samantha froze. Her blood chilled and flowed more slowly, bumping into floes of fear as she began to realize the dimension of Blanding's madness.

He reentered the room. "I bought you some more of your favorites, dear." He was carrying a pitcher of iced tea and, holding it by the string, a box of animal crackers. His sword clanked as he moved.

He patted her on the shoulder. "Sit. Sit down and we'll have our tea party." He opened the little box with the circus animals pictured on the outside. "I'll find you the elephants," he said. "I know they're your favorites."

"They taste better," Sam said very softly. Maybe she could get through this if she played along.

"You always say that," Blanding said, and laughed. It was the first time she'd seen him smile. His complexion pinkened, came alive. He had a beautiful smile.

"What have you been doing today," he asked, "while I was at the store?"

Sam hesitated.

"Have you been visiting with Mrs. Brown again?"

She nodded.

"I do think it's nice that you keep one another company. Especially with her being such high society. Imagine, both the mother *and* wife of governors."

"Imagine." She didn't have a clue.

"Though she has nothing on you, my dear. Don't think I meant that for a moment." Blanding reached over and stroked Sam's curls. "And I don't think that portrait of her on her gravestone is particularly flattering. Do you?"

"No, I don't." Sam shifted in her chair as she began to get his drift.

"Can you imagine, her going to all that trouble to order her own gravestone on that Grand Tour, and then coming home with such an unfortunate likeness? I think the simple inscription I chose for you is much more tasteful. Don't you?"

Sam choked on a sip of iced tea. "Yes—oh, yes."

"I'm sorry it'll soon be time for you to be getting back. We'll have to put you under again before you're missed."

Sam pictured beautiful old Oakland Cemetery up

the hill, the resting place of many of Atlanta's early elite. What an interesting idea of Blanding's, the dead visiting together: his wife and Mrs. Brown; Margaret Mitchell chatting up mayors and generals; slaves and paupers sitting down with Morris Rich, the founder of the city's famous department stores, or the golfer Bobby Jones. But the Coca-Cola Candlers wouldn't be at an Oakland tête à tête. For that family, the elite of the elite, had long ago bought Westview Cemetery and moved the right side of the tracks to the other side of town, causing entire crypts of other families to be dismantled and moved there from Oakland, society wishing to stay as close to the Candlers, so the wags said, in death as in life.

Sam looked up. Herman Blanding was standing now with a frown on his face, cleaning an old muzzle-loader. She started. Was he going to shoot her now that they'd had tea?

"I'm going to kill the son-of-a-bitch who did this to you," he growled. At his feet, General Lee muttered sympathetically.

"He's in jail. Carlos Ortega is in jail," Sam said softly, hoping to remind him that the murderer of his wife, Susan, had been put away.

"No, no, no!" Blanding twisted his head, his teeth holding the string of a bag of gunpowder. "Ortega was the instrument. Like this rifle"—he patted it—"is the instrument of my vengeance. I'm going to kill Forrest Ridley!"

Samantha was about to tell him that Ridley was already dead, but then she remembered that Blanding had been at his funeral. On some level, he had to know that.

"They're the scourge of the earth, lawyers,"

Blanding fumed, his face growing more and more livid. He waved a finger in her face. "We should shoot them! Shoot them on sight! Come here." He pulled on her arm. "Come, Miss Adams. I have something to show you."

Well, at least he once again knew who she was.

He propelled her through the surprisingly neat kitchen and out the back door into a tiny backyard. There, beyond a patch of a freshly tilled vegetable garden, plastered against the side of a toolshed, were life-size blowups of the head of Forrest Ridley. Sam recognized the photograph as the one that had appeared in the *Constitution* with Ridley's obituary. A peppering of holes had been blasted through the eyes until they were sievelike.

"Watch," Blanding whispered, laying a finger alongside his nose as if they were partners in a conspiracy.

He stepped inside the door of the toolshed, and as he flipped a switch, the eyes of Forrest Ridley glowed red.

"Do you like it?" Blanding cackled, then stuck his head back out of the shed, grinning. "Doesn't that make him look like the devil, that little red light?"

Leaving the light burning, he rejoined her beside the tiny plot of tilled earth.

"See that?" He pointed. Over in one corner of the yard was a small wooden cross. "He did that, too."

"What, Herman?"

"Killed my Sheba, General Lee's mother."

The dog's ears perked up at the mention of his name.

"Forrest Ridley killed your dog?"

"Nawh." He waved away the specificity of her question as if it were unimportant. "But another one just like him did. Defended the son-of-a-bitch who ran over her. I went to court. Yes sirree. You bet I did. Went to court and sued the son-of-a-bitch, but that oily devil, that *lawyer"*—he spat the word—"he got him off scot-free. Never had to pay me a dime. Laughed, that's what they did. Laughed in my face in the courtroom. Son-of-a-bitch laughed at me."

"But not Ridley?" Sam asked softly.

Blanding drew his sword. Sam stepped back. But he brandished it in the air above his head, looking to the life like the famous portrait of John Brown, wild-eyed, crazy.

"Kill them all!" he shouted. "Sons-of-bitches are the earth's scourge. Pestilence! Damnation!"

Then he took Sam's hand in his free one. "Pray with me," he said hoarsely, emotion shaking in his voice. "Pray with me for Forrest Ridley's death."

This time she tried reminding him. "Herman, you know he's already dead."

"Hallelujah!" he shouted. "Praise the Lord! Vengeance is mine, saith the Lord! Thank you, oh Lord. Thank you, Jesus."

He dropped his sword and grasped both her hands. "Sing with me," he said. "Sing with me, Miss Samantha Adams."

And then, in a childlike voice, high-pitched, he sang a song she remembered from Sunday School many years ago.

"What a friend we have in Jesus," he crooned. "All our sins and griefs to bear." Tears gathered in his eyes. "What a friend we have in Jesus. Take it to the Lord in prayer."

He smiled into her face, his beautiful, gentle, crazed smile. "He's answered my prayers, Miss Samantha.

He's sent someone to kill them all." Then he crossed his arms over his chest and turned his head in a gesture of supplication. "Not me. No, not me. He did not find me worthy. But someone. Someone stronger and more valiant. Someone worthy of the task."

He turned and smiled at General Lee. "Come, boy," he said. The powerful dog jumped to attention. "We've got to ready ourselves for the battle. They're coming. They're coming to try to take the railroad now. We've got to stop them. It's our duty, die if we must, to save Atlanta, to save the South!"

He began to march around the small garden plot, General Lee following close behind, his bearing as military as a dog's can be.

"Look to the north," Blanding called to Sam as she slipped toward the side of the house and her departure. "Look to the lines at Peachtree Creek. That's where the battle will be joined. We'll ride like hell to help you at the creek when we're done here. We'll smash the vipers as they crawl out of their nests. To the north!" He flashed his sword once more. "The North is where the devil lives."

Eleven

——————◆——————

CLIMBING BACK INTO HER CAR, SHE THOUGHT, I'D GIVE anything to stop in at Manuel's for a cold one. Herman Blanding had knocked her for a loop.

Samantha drove back north on Highland. She could see ahead that the roadblock had been cleared, but instead of proceeding on to the address in Virginia-Highland Lona had given her, she wheeled into Manuel's parking lot, stepped inside, and ordered up a frosty glass of the diet version of Atlanta's official drink, a Coca-Cola. It wasn't bad with peanuts.

She sat at the bar staring at her reflection in the mirror behind the bar and thought about calling Beau. Had Horace delivered to him the fingerprints he said he'd get from Lona?

But she knew that Horace would do as he'd promised. Horace was as reliable as the rising sun.

That wasn't why she wanted to call Beau. It was the dream she'd had about him last night. Damn him, why had he moved back home?

In the dream, Beau and she, both very young, were

135

floating on the surface of a lake in a rowboat. She was wearing a yellow sundress. He leaned over and pinned a fragrant gardenia in her hair. Then time shifted, and they were sitting on the edge of a cot in a boathouse. Beau untied the little straps of her sundress very slowly, looking all the while into her eyes in the glow of a kerosene lantern. She let the top of her dress drop. He murmured something she couldn't quite make out and then lowered his head. But his head was silver, as now. They weren't young. His lips, soft as pansy petals, lowered to her breast.

"I said, ''Scuse me, could you pass the salt?'"

Sam jumped. A stranger seated at her right elbow was grinning at her.

"Sorry. I was daydreaming."

"No problem." He kept grinning. He was a handsome good old boy, a country boy come to town and prosperity, a salesman sporting a diamond pinky ring that glittered when he raised the hard-boiled egg in his left hand. His right hugged a beer.

"What's a pretty lady like you doing here sitting all alone drinking a Co'-Cola? Can I buy you something else?"

"No, thank you," she said, and then pulled out the line she used for these occasions when she didn't want to be bothered—which she usually didn't, resenting the attentions of presumptuous strangers: "I'm an alcoholic."

"Well, hell," he said, turning to the man on his right and including him, "we all got our little faults, ain't we? Like my friend Chester here." Then he stuck out his hand toward her. "I'm Eugene." The two men smiled, and lit up the bar.

She had to smile back. Ease up, she told herself.

They're just being friendly—like Labradors. That's what they looked like, both big and muscular with short haircuts, smooth necks—sleek, boisterous, teenage dogs. She introduced herself.

"Chester," Eugene continued, "now, his little fault, he cain't help himself, he goes out into the country once a month and bays at the moon."

Wolf, Labrador. She was close.

"I guess that's harmless enough," she said, laughing.

"Well, it would be, if he didn't fall in love with cows. Scares the bejesus out of 'em, him trotting along on all fours at their heels. Plays hell on the farmer, too—makes the milk clabber."

"You a fine one to talk," Chester defended himself. "Your whole family is damned Fruit Loops."

"Now, is that a nice way to talk in front of this young lady I'm trying to impress?" Eugene protested.

"Might not. But it's the truth. Tell her about your Uncle Moses, boy."

"Lord have mercy, Chester. You gone bring that tired old thing up?"

But Sam thought he was protesting too much, and she was right, because Eugene immediately ordered up another round and launched into what had to be one of his favorite stories.

"My Uncle Moses, see, he's the mayor of this little town, Towunda, down in south Georgia, where all the folks are crazy 'cause they're descended from those criminals Oglethorpe brought over."

"Not to mention the incest and the fluoridation," Chester interrupted. "Course, Gene's from Albany" —he pronounced it "Al*biny*"—"which ain't too far from there."

"Which makes me crazy, too. I never said I wuddn't. *Anyway,* as I was about to say before I was so rudely interrupted, my Uncle Moses was slap silly about his daughter B.J., short for Bobbie June. He and Aunt May Lou'd had six sons before Bobbie June came along, when Aunt May Lou said 'Praise the Lord' and kicked him out of her bedroom, but anyway B.J. was the apple of his eye. She got to be the princess of Towunda when she was growing up.

"What with Uncle Moses being the mayor, why, anything that little girl wanted, all she had to do was point. They had a school play, she was the star. They had a dance recital, she took the last and longest bows. They had a drawing at the Piggly Wiggly for a sack of groceries, Moses would show up with Bobbie June in tow, and no matter whose name they drew, they was smart enough to give the sack to Bobbie June. 'Cause you didn't want to get on the wrong side of Uncle Moses about his daughter. If you did, next thing you knew you'd get your car impounded, your livestock locked up; no end of trouble could come to sit on your front porch and visit you.

"Anyway, my Uncle Moses looks like the south end of a mule headed north, whereas Aunt May Lou is a nice-looking woman. Luckily, the good Lord made it so B.J. favored Aunt May Lou's side. In fact, He did them one better, because by the time B.J. was about fifteen, why, she was a raving beauty. Wuddn't she, Chester?"

"You can say that again. Miss America didn't have nothing on her. Blond hair, big blue eyes, cherry lips, and besides, she was built—pardon me, Samantha— but B.J. was built even then like a brick shithouse. She was worth the special trip I made down from

Athens—that's where me and this old boy met, up at school—to see her. Course, it was too late by then."

"Now, don't be giving away the story, Bubba. This here's mine. You got one to tell, you just wait your turn," Eugene said.

"'*Scuse* me, partner. Go on ahead."

"Anyway, as I was saying, B.J. was something else. She'd been homecoming queen three years running, which has never happened before or since in the history of Towunda High School, when all of a sudden, in her senior year, everything just went to hell."

"Say what?" Sam said, then caught herself. Well, it didn't take long, did it, for her to sound as if she'd never left home.

"See, Uncle Moses had never let her go out with boys, *not once,* but when it got to be her senior year, well, Aunt May Lou put her foot down," Eugene continued.

"'Moses,' she says, 'that child is going to grow up an old maid if you're not careful. She's never going to leave home.'

"'That's exactly what I'm planning on,' says Moses. 'You think I'm ever going to let those horny hounds coming sniffing around my sweetheart, you got another think coming.'

"Well, of course, Uncle Moses couldn't watch B.J. twenty-four hours a day, what with he had his mayoring and his feed and seed store to look after, so Aunt May Lou let her start stepping out when Uncle Moses wasn't around.

"I guess all the yearning in B.J. had built up too long, because right after Christmas she turned up pregnant. Aunt May Lou could have shipped her off to relatives to have the baby, which is what most nice folks did in this kind of situation, but not without telling Uncle Moses. He would no more have let his baby girl out of his sight for the five or six months it would have taken than he would have shot himself in the foot.

"So Aunt May Lou got him drunk one night and told him the bad news. He *stayed* drunk for three or four days. Then when he finally sobered up, he loaded his shotgun, bound and determined to shoot the son-of-a-bitch who had ruined his darling sweetheart. The problem was, he didn't know who to shoot, because Bobbie June wasn't telling. No matter how he bribed her, how he begged her, she wouldn't say squat.

"Aunt May Lou went right ahead with plans for the wedding. Holding her head just as high as she always had in her position as Miz Mayor of Towunda, she ordered off to the Saks Fifth Avenue for B.J.'s wedding dress—and for the dresses of the twelve brides-maids, all in descending shades of pink. She said that no matter what, this was going to be one wedding that Towunda wouldn't forget."

"She was sure right about that," Chester added.

Eugene scowled, waited a minute to see if Chester was through interrupting, then went on.

"Well, the day approached for the wedding, B.J. getting bigger all the time because thirteen custom-order dresses from Saks Fifth Avenue took a while, but Aunt May Lou said it didn't make no never mind, because everybody in town knew what was going on; it was how *pretty* the wedding was that mattered at this point.

"As the day got closer, Uncle Moses came unglued.

He started posting himself out at the city limits sign, out by the truck stop, and when the brown UPS truck hove into sight, Uncle Moses would pull out into the highway with his honorary sireen blasting and take possession of it."

"You mean he took the driver's money?" asked Sam incredulously.

"Hell, no. It was the packages he was after. He figured if the dresses never came, then there wouldn't *be* any wedding."

"He'd rather B.J. was an unwed mother?"

"He didn't care about that. He'd raise the baby, no problem, just as long as B.J. stayed home."

"And all this time B.J. hadn't named the father?"

"Nope. You'd have thought that girl's mouth was stuck with Crazy Glue," Eugene said with satisfaction.

"Did the father of the baby know that he was getting married?"

"Well, I'm getting to that part. See, after a while, even though Uncle Moses was the mayor of Towunda, the sheriff had to take matters into his own hands and lock Uncle Moses up every day from noon to one so the UPS man could get through."

"Wasn't the sheriff afraid of Uncle Moses?"

"Well, he sure as hell wasn't comfortable about the whole thing, but a little town like Towunda, people sort of depend on their deliveries. I mean, it ain't just stuff from fancy Saks Fifth Avenue that was coming on that truck. There was Sears and Penney's and Monkey Ward. People were starting to get mean about not getting their washing machines parts, their new microwave ovens, and their tennis shoes. So they took up a petition about Moses, much as they liked him, and there wasn't much else the sheriff could do. Besides which, the UPS was getting hot under the collar, and they said if the sheriff didn't do something about Uncle Moses, they was going to cut Towunda off the route permanently.

"So it got to be a routine. Sheriff Bailey would come over to the feed and seed store every day, shake Uncle Moses' hand, and then lock him up. Had lunch already ordered for him, one day from the Hardee's, the next from the McDonald's. But mostly he ordered from the Pig 'n Whistle, Uncle Moses' favorite blue-plate special barbecue."

"Why didn't Uncle Moses try to hide?" Sam asked. She was on her third Coca-Cola by now and felt like soon her teeth were going to float, but she couldn't leave the bar—especially now that Eugene seemed to be closing in on the good part.

"He did hide out a couple of times, but it didn't do no good. See, everybody knew where he was headed, and all they had to do was wait for him out by the city limits sign.

"Bunch of folks did that very thing one day when he gave Bailey the slip, and it was embarrassing for Moses to have an audience when Bailey put him in the sheriff's car, even if he did sit up front and turn on the blue light himself, and even if they did yell encouragements to him, like 'Go on ahead, Moses.'

"So anyway, the great day came when the dresses got through, though by that time B.J. had grown so big they had to let out all the seams in hers and then sew in some stretchy lace around the middle.

"Course, nobody told Uncle Moses the dresses had come. Aunt May Lou had made an arrangement with Sheriff Bailey, who just kept on locking Uncle Moses up for lunch till it was Saturday and they could hold the wedding. So Moses is sitting in his cell, chewing on a pork rib like any other day, when all of a sudden the bells of the First Baptist Church, which is right across the street from the jail, cut loose. And two minutes later you can hear old Miz Pringle pumping away at "Here Comes the Bride" on the organ at an extra-fast tempo, like she needed to hurry up and get home and check on something she'd left in the oven.

"Uncle Moses gets all bug-eyed as he figures it out, 'cause he may be stubborn, which is where B.J. got hers from, but he ain't stupid. And just like Superman —I mean, they have never figured out yet exactly how he got out of that cell, and Sheriff Bailey is too embarrassed to this day to talk about it—but Moses busted out. Just tore loose.

"He ran down them front steps, across the street, up the steps of the church, and he almost made it in, too, but Preacher Barlow saw him coming from up at the pulpit and yelled right out in the middle of the ceremony, 'Boys, lock them doors!' And the deacons standing in the back, who were well trained, did what they were told to."

"So *who* was she marrying?" Sam asked, squirming with impatience and because she had to go to the bathroom.

"Well, that's the thing. Nobody knew. She wouldn't tell *anybody*, not even Aunt May Lou. So what May Lou had done was she ordered, on pain of death and tar-and-feathering, for every single male in town who was between the ages of fourteen and fifty-four to be there and be square and look presentable. It was sort of like a sweepstakes—nobody knew who was going to win."

"Or lose," said Sam.

"Well, no, I don't think any of them thought of it that way. I mean, it had gotten to be such an exciting thing, you know, that you'd just be proud to be pointed out as the daddy. And marrying B.J. would have been a treat. I mean, she *was* a beauty. She kinda reminded you of pink spun-sugar candy at the country fair. You know, the kind that was so soft and sweet that you just never could get enough in your mouth at once.

"So anyway, every man that was eligible and some that wasn't was sitting up there combed and curried within an inch of their lives, hoping against hope, even if they'd never said more than howdy-do to B.J., that they'd be the one."

Eugene paused for a second as the bartender set down another round.

"You have to understand," he continued after a long pull on his beer, "that Towunda is about as big as this room, and there's not too much excitement there in the day to day, or even in the year to year."

"Or millennium to millennium," Chester threw in fast.

"So there they all are. B.J.'s down at the front now, having walked down the aisle behind all those graduated pink bridesmaids on the arm of Aunt May Lou, who was in deep rose and looking just as pleased as punch that she'd pulled this thing off. And the preacher had inserted this extra little line into the ceremony, something like, 'Would the bride please take the hand of her intended,' at which B.J. was going to reach out into the congregation and grab ahold of the lucky man.

"Everybody's just sitting there on pins and needles,

and just as the preacher says it and B.J. takes a long, slow look around the church, *kerwham!* There was this crash that sounded like kingdom come.

"Uncle Moses had gone and gotten in his brand-new Cadillac El Dorado and driven it around and around the square, building up momentum, and at that moment he steered it right through the First Baptist's front doors. He jumps out of the car waving his shotgun and yelling, 'Show me the son-of-a-bitch!' and B.J. screams, 'Oh, my God!' and stares down at the floor under all that white lace, because her water had broke. She went into labor right then and there, but they did manage to get her home before she was delivered of an eight-and-a-half-pound premature baby boy."

"Premature," Sam said, laughing, "because she still wasn't married."

"That's right." Eugene grinned. "And she still ain't, till this very day."

"Are you kidding?"

"Would I tease about a thing like that? She said, 'Hell, I got this far. Now I already *am* an unwed mother. Guess it don't make no difference now, so forget the whole thing.' Named the boy Moses Junior, and stayed home just like her daddy wanted in the first place.

"Course, she slips around from time to time, but she's careful about taking care of business, now that she's grown up, so there've been no more little Moses Juniors to worry about. Her daddy gave her a red El Dorado of her very own for graduation when she went back that next fall and finished school. And she and May Lou go off shopping to New York whenever the spirit moves them. Bring the things right home with them. Don't have to wait for the UPS. They all live right there in Towunda together, just as happy as if they had good sense."

"I don't believe it," Sam said. She stood up and headed toward the ladies' room, then stopped and turned. "Eugene, who *was* the father of that child?"

Eugene slapped Chester on the back, and they both laughed.

"That's the best part," Eugene said. "See, I got B.J. drunk one night a couple of years later and asked her the same thing, and she said, 'You know, Gene, Daddy came busting through that door just in the nick of time. I didn't know what the hell I was going to do. When Mama let me start going out, I was like a pig in shit. Didn't spend one ounce of discretion. I had myself a quandary there, pointing out who the father was, 'cause I didn't have a clue.'"

"You're lying, Eugene," Sam accused, hands on her hips. "You've made this whole thing up."

"Well, honey," Eugene answered, chuckling, "them's the chances you take when you drink Co'-Colas in bars with strangers. Ain't it, Chester? I guess the answer to that's for me to know"—he winked at her—"and you to find out."

Twelve

◆

WELL, JUST LIKE OLD B.J., YOU DON'T HAVE A CLUE either, do you, Sam said to herself as she pulled out of Manuel's parking lot. You've spent the whole morning talking to a crazy man who's threatening to kill Forrest Ridley because he can't even remember Ridley is already dead, drinking Coca-Colas, and listening to shaggy dog stories. You're no closer to whoever murdered Forrest Ridley, *if* anyone murdered Forrest Ridley, than you ever were. Maybe you ought to get on the horn and call Hoke and turn yourself in.

"Save me from myself, Hoke," she said aloud. "Send me to cover a garbage strike. I'm an investigative incompetent."

She would no more do that than she'd admit that there was nothing to her corrupt sheriff story—which she might never know, if she didn't hurry up and get around to it.

Sam stopped at the intersection of Virginia and Highland. This was the most walkable shopping neighborhood in a town addicted to automobiles and malls, a cluster of clever restaurants and antique/scented soap/record shops. But she'd overshot her destination. She turned the car around, pulled into a parking spot, and reached for the street map that every native carried, except those who liked driving in circles.

Atlanta, Sam thought, had to be one of the most confusing cities on earth. Streets changed names at will; there were fourteen variants on Peachtree, from Avenue to Valley, not to mention the fabled Peachtree Street, the main artery which in its travels north and south crossed Piedmont Avenue three times, which ought to be an impossibility. There were no grids, no straight lines, neither rhyme nor reason to the patterning. One simply memorized pathways through the city and, at all times, carried that map.

Sam pulled her map out of the glove compartment. Damn! she thought. Virginia Circle didn't come through. She traced the path she needed to take with her finger. Back to Virginia, then a right turn, next a left, and another quick left, and there the street was.

Virginia-Highland was a close-in neighborhood of 1920s bungalows. Allowed to grow seedy, the area had started to rejuvenate in the late seventies. Armed with bright paints and imagination, new young homeowners began to refurbish the broad-hipped, comfortable old houses and fill their yards and driveways with baby carriages and BMWs. Less than three miles from the center of the city, the area was a nice walk across Piedmont Park from the Ansley Park neighborhood.

A nice, long, leisurely walk, thought Sam, for a man and his dog.

She found Virginia Circle, then drove slowly, looking at the numbers: 198, 200, 204. She had passed the house. She backed up. No wonder. The lot that was 202, the number Lona had written on the piece of notepaper Sam was holding, was screened by tall overgrown hedges at the street and looked like part of the next-door neighbor's yard.

Sam parked and walked cautiously down the cracked driveway. A blue cornflower blossomed through the cement. She crept up the front steps. In the mailbox were only supermarket fliers and advertisements for a tire sale. She circled the small house. All the blinds were tightly pulled.

Pulling her wallet out of her purse, Sam scanned her credit cards and chose the brown Saks card. This one's for you, Bobbie June, she told herself. Slipping it into the back door, she jiggled the doorknob as Sean had taught her. The door swung wide.

It was like a dollhouse, the kind she had always imagined she'd like to live in when she grew old— neat, self-contained, without a lot of fuss and bother.

The fifties kitchen was spotless, all white, except for shiny new yellow floor tiles. There was no sign that anyone lived here, except for a glass coffeemaker on the back of the range. The countertops were bare, though the cupboards revealed a few dishes, coffee cups, wine and champagne glasses, and a box of Sweet 'n Low.

The refrigerator was a different matter. Neatly stacked inside were a dozen bottles of extra-dry Perrier-Jouet champagne. On one shelf was a bag of Blue Mountain Jamaican coffee. In the freezer Sam found containers of chocolate and vanilla Häagen-Dazs ice cream and Gold Brick chocolate sauce.

The living room was absolutely empty, as was the

first bedroom. The second bedroom, however, was a storyteller.

A king-size bed almost filled it. Beneath a white fur throw were sheets of sleek white satin. In the drawer of the bedside table, the only other piece of furniture in the room, were a couple of joints, a roach clip, and an unopened bar of Lindt dark chocolate with hazelnuts. Behind the chocolate was a vibrator, its cord neatly wrapped.

In the bathroom was a collection of toothbrushes in various colors, a tube of toothpaste, and, across the back of the tub, loofah sponges and a set of soaps, oils, and gels—all Chanel No. 5. Stacks of new thick white towels filled the small linen closet.

That was it. No clothes. No pictures. No letters. Only the faint fragrance of Chanel and, as Sam closed her eyes for a moment, the smell of sex.

"The place has got to be full of prints. Did you touch anything?" Beau asked.

Sam didn't answer.

"Sure you did. That's okay. We can separate yours out."

"The note?"

"It's slow going. Horace brought over Queen and Liza and Lona's prints. But it's going to take a long while to see if there's anything else there."

"So what we'll find here are Forrest Ridley's prints and a woman's."

Then she heard what she'd just said. Who was this "we"? He'd done it. He'd known the quest would get the better of her, that it would be no trick at all to worm his way in.

"Sounds like it. Sure sounds like a love nest." He

paused for a long moment. "Chocolate sauce, huh? And satin sheets? Tell me again what was in the bedside drawer."

"I forget."

"Then maybe we need to go over there together and take a closer look."

"Do it yourself. I've got more important things on my agenda, like driving up to Monroeville."

"Not a good idea, Sam. Nothing up there for you. Dodd's not gonna tell you a thing. You after him because you think he's implicated in the Ridley case? Or is he just one of your sheriffs? You still pursuing that story?"

"Well, it would sure be tidy if he were both, wouldn't it?"

"Wouldn't it? Not damn likely, though. Lightning doesn't strike twice, you know."

"I want to go see the falls for myself."

"Want me to drive you up?"

"You never stop, do you?"

"Not till I get what I want. Nope."

Thirteen

GEORGE GRINNED WHEN SAM TOLD HIM ABOUT THE Virginia Circle bungalow.

"Didn't know Ridley had it in him. Sounds like a place I'd have created myself in my younger days."

Horace entered carrying a tray of ham sandwiches, potato salad, iced tea, and a dark beer for George. "Don't you remember that place over on Baltimore Place that you and Mr. Thompson once took on shares?"

"Hush! Samantha doesn't need to know what a gay blade I was."

"And still are." Peaches delivered her line as she passed down the hallway and kept going.

"You're talking about an old man who's half-blind," George called after her. "How can I be chasing if I can't even see?"

"Don't need to see to feel. 'Specially when you don't have to chase very hard. Or very far." Peaches' voice trailed off down the hall.

Sam fixed her gaze on her uncle, who was now

152

savoring his first sip of the cold dark beer. She didn't know anything about his romantic life, except that when he was young, he'd been married briefly to a beautiful woman with chestnut hair named Eloise. Her picture sat in a cloisonné frame on the baby grand piano. Eloise, his childhood sweetheart and the love of George's life, had died giving birth to their first son, who was stillborn.

"It took him ages," Peaches had told Sam, "to even be able to say her name."

But that had been more than forty years ago, and the tall, dapper George Adams, whose beautiful Egyptian cotton shirts, dark suits, summer linens, and seersuckers all came from Savile Row, grew, as some men do, more handsome each year. His figure was no longer slim, but even his heft was becoming. His dark curls had turned pure white. Those clear blue eyes remained the same as in the old photos Samantha had looked at, only the laugh lines at the corners deepened. Had he not been her kin, she herself would have found him appealing. It didn't surprise her to hear Horace and Peaches hinting that other women did.

"George, why is it you never talk to me about your women friends?" she asked.

"Well . . ." He paused and wiped his mouth with a linen napkin. "I guess I just think that those things are best left unsaid."

"But—"

He raised a hand. "If I plan to run off with any showgirls, I'll let you know."

They both laughed.

"Now," he said, "let's talk about what I've been able to find out for you about Watkin County. You're still set on going up there?"

"Tomorrow morning, bright and early."

"This should give you something to think about." He pulled out the notes he'd taken in his now-huge printed hand. He had taken to using children's wide-ruled school pads as his eyesight dimmed. "I told you I was curious about land development up there. There's lots of money, I mean big sums, changing hands."

Sam nodded and picked up Harpo, who had scooted into the room. He snuggled into her lap, turning so she could scratch his ears.

"Well, it was just as I expected. In Watkin County, the sheriff and the tax commissioner are one and the same. So obviously the sheriff knows when land is being sold at auction for taxes. He runs a tiny notice in the paper in practically invisible two-point type, and when the day comes, nobody shows up at the auction except the sheriff and the real estate agent or lawyer with whom he's in cahoots."

"And who's that man?"

"Jeb Saunders."

"You know him?"

"I sure do. He has an association with Simmons and Lee."

"Which points the finger at whom? Forrest Ridley? Is that why he was killed? Land deals?"

"No, not Forrest. What's interesting is what my man—"

"Who?" Sam demanded.

"Let's just say that some of the firm's young associates are awfully eager and can find their way around courthouse records like they're on roller skates, if given the motivation. Anyway, my young man found

the name of Kay Kramer on many of the recent
Watkin land deeds. Kay Kramer and Patricia Kay."

"Kay Kay?"

"Kramer's her maiden name."

"And Patricia?"

"Totsie."

"The Kay women are tied up in this?" Sam asked
incredulously.

"No. I don't think so. I think Edison just used their
names as fronts."

"I never did like that man. Do you?"

"Well, just because we were partners didn't mean
we got into bed together, if you know what I mean."

"But did you suspect him of this kind of thing?"
Sam pressed.

"Not suspect, exactly. But I'll tell you, it's no great
surprise. The man's greedy. You can see it in his
eyes."

"So, when's the next sale? Did your young man find
that out?"

There was silence from George's end of the room.

"Don't con a conman," Sam told him. "I learned
everything I know from you. And I know when you're
holding out. Give."

"Tomorrow."

"Hot damn! What timing! I ask you." Sam stood,
despite Harpo's grumblings, and strode around the
room. "This is great. I'll go and see it at first hand."

"You don't know these people, Samantha. I keep
telling you you don't want to mess with them. They
play hardball."

"That's all I've heard since I started talking about
this rural sheriff idea. And you're the one who turned

me on to it in the first place. Now, it just so happens that we've got a sheriff—certainly corrupt, and maybe implicated in Forrest Ridley's death—and you're telling me to lay off? Forget it, George. Daylight tomorrow, I'm gone."

George smiled at her back as she walked out the door, followed close behind by Harpo.

She was the child he'd never had. And he was fearful for her. But in her place, he knew he'd have done exactly what she was doing. Nose right on the trail, hang the consequences.

Headed north and slightly east on Route 400, Sam crossed the perimeter highway a little after nine, Peaches having insisted despite her protestations that Sam could not set foot out the door without a proper breakfast.

At the last minute she'd scooped up Harpo, who had been watching her every move before settling down with his resigned and grumpy look, his lower teeth slightly protruding.

"You want to go, Scooter?"

The little dog had danced in a circle. *Go* was his middle name. Now he was settled in her lap, happily snoozing as the miles rolled by.

The suburbs seemed to stretch on forever. George was right: Atlanta was marching northward out of Fulton County and into Forsyth. Sign after sign by the side of the highway announced subdivisions with names like Arrowwood and Bowling Green—little enclaves of tract housing with all the authenticity of Disney World.

Sam remembered then something that Beau told her his daughter Beth had said. Once when they were driving up this way, she'd asked, "Dad, what is this all *for?*"

Sam, who'd always preferred living in the thick of things, wasn't sure.

Once off the expressway and onto two-lane Route 19, she left the suburbs behind. This was a land of piney woods and rolling hills that, another county northward, became the Appalachians' toes. It was kudzu country, where that creeping vine imported from Japan to prevent erosion indiscriminately covered hills and trees, old cars, abandoned houses, and, some said, sleeping cows—its heart-shaped leaves prettily disguising its voraciousness.

Huge chicken coops filled some roadside lots, the results of a new form of sharecropping as the big growers provided the farmers with chicks and feed in exchange for most of the full-grown birds that would later fill supermarket coolers.

This was the sort of land into which Herman Blanding's house would blend comfortably, Sam thought, where a front yard filled with old trucks, skeletons of station wagons, rusting lawn furniture, and a big television satellite dish was the rule rather than the exception. New double-wide mobile homes were erected right beside tumbledown shacks, the occupants sliding the latter's contents right over into the former without missing a beat. It was a land where Christmas trees were farmed, as well as gourds and serious timber. It was all-white country, these "sundown" counties where blacks were not welcome after dark. It was provincial, parochial, and overwhelmingly Protestant. A sign on a Baptist church Sam passed read: *Are you a runaway from God? Please call home.* And it was poor country. Though the land was beautiful, it didn't bring its inhabitants wealth—except recently, to a select few, when large parcels of it were sold.

Sam approached the Monroeville city limits leaning into a roller-coaster curve called Long Pond Bend. She loved the way her car hugged the road. Harpo awakened and licked her hand. He was a great traveler.

"Good boy," she said. "You can get out in just a moment."

In that moment she was in the town's center, and if she'd kept driving for another, she would have been through it. Monroeville was just about a fifteen-second town if you were doing twenty, which was what the speed limit allowed.

There in the middle of the road was the old courthouse Beau had described, two-storied and crumbling a bit like a jilted bride's wedding cake. Other than that, there was no real center to the town, not even a block-long parade of stores, but here and there were a fuel company, a tiny library, a poolroom, a florist, three new-looking gas stations, and a Qwik-Stop grocery store. Off on the one little street that intersected the highway was a window with gold-leaf letters announcing it to be the office of Jeb Saunders, the lawyer whom George had indicated was arm-in-arm with Sheriff Dodd.

On the other side of the road, down in a gully, was the new white-brick courthouse, standing out like a bottle blonde. Sam walked down that way. Harpo raised his leg against the tire of a brown Ford, a Watkin County Sheriff's patrol car. Behind the courthouse she could see the county jail, its windows barred. To one side of it was an exercise yard with a horseshoe pit. If that was the extent of the recreational activity, Sam thought, serving time in Watkin County must be terrifically boring. To one side of the door to the sheriff's office was a Pepsi-Cola machine. A tall, chunky man in a brown uniform standing in front of it looked up and smiled.

"How you?" he said.

"Fine."

It had taken her a while to acclimate again to the friendly ways of Southerners. They waved, tipped their hats, made small polite conversation with any stranger who passed. It was quite a contrast to San Francisco, where people slid by one another avoiding eye contact.

"Nice morning," he continued, then peered at Harpo. "Pardon me, ma'am, but what kind of dog is that?"

"A Shih Tzu."

"Well, I never saw nothing like it."

"He's Chinese."

"Beg your pardon?"

"Chinese. The breed's Chinese."

The man tipped his hat back and studied Harpo, who studied him back. Harpo gave great eye contact.

"If he's Chinese," the man said after a while, "how come his eyes ain't slanted?" And then he slapped his knee and broke up laughing at his own joke.

"Pretty funny," Sam agreed. "Tell me, where could I get a cup of coffee around here?"

"Up at Millie's." He pointed north. "Just on the other side of the old courthouse. You can't miss it."

"Thank you, sir. Come on, Harpo." Harpo resisted

her pull on the leash. He had an eyelock on the deputy, as if he were still trying to figure out what the man thought was so funny. Harpo had a well-defined sense of humor, but he didn't get the man's joke. Sam had to pick him up and carry him away.

Sam was hoping that Millie's would be a homey kind of place like the Silver Skillet or Melvin's, but it wasn't. It was new plastic from top to bottom, though the pie in the case and the clientele looked homemade enough.

She took a seat at the counter, which was almost full, though the booths were all empty, then twirled around toward the plate glass window to check on Harpo, whom she'd locked in the car. He was staring indignantly at her from behind the steering wheel.

"What can I get you?"

Sam turned, but she couldn't find the owner of the voice. Then she looked down. The waitress was a red-haired midget about four feet tall.

Sam didn't blink. "A cup of coffee, please."

At that, the other heads at the counter, all male, turned, stared politely, and nodded. She and the waitress seemed to be the only two women in Monroeville who didn't drink their morning coffee at home.

"You traveling?" asked the old man on her right, who was dressed in a khaki workshirt and matching pants. His cigarette never moved from his mouth, not even when he sipped his coffee.

"I am," she said with a smile. "Drove up from Atlanta. I understand there's a lot of pretty land up here for sale. Thought I might be interested in a big parcel for a summer place."

"Humph," said the old man, nudging his neighbor

with his right elbow. "Reckon we don't know about summer places. We work our land all four seasons."

Sam smiled weakly. What a dummy she was. "Well," she repeated, "it is awfully pretty. You know of any for sale?"

"Nope." The man shook his head. "Don't reckon I do. Do you, Willis?"

His neighbor shook his head even as he buried his face in a plate of pancakes.

"Well, when land does come up for sale, do you have any idea how much it would sell for per acre?" Sam persisted.

"Nope."

Giving up on him, Sam tried a smile on the man to her left, a young man who had a creaky look as if life had sucked all of the juice out of him.

Before she could even reframe the question he joined the chorus: "Nope."

"Well, if a person *was* ever to buy some land up here, is there anyplace that you could fly a small plane into? I mean, if you wanted to fly up from Atlanta instead of drive?"

The three men exchanged glances across her. Even without looking, she could feel their lines of silent communication as clearly as if they were darts.

She *knew* she shouldn't have asked that. It was far too obviously a question about drugs. Stick to it, Sam, she lectured herself. Just like George told you, you go on an unfocused fishing expedition up here, you may come up with things more wiggly than worms.

"Nope." They shook their heads in three-part harmony. "Nope. Nope."

Well, this certainly has been an informative little cup of coffee, Sam thought. She could have learned just as much by sitting in the car drinking from her thermos and talking with Harpo. She motioned for her check and paid up.

Halfway out to her car, she heard someone calling after her.

"Miss, miss, you left your paper."

It was the waitress. She shifted from side to side above her short legs as she descended the diner's steps.

"Thanks. You needn't have bothered."

"There's an old landing strip from World War II about three miles east of town," the woman said, and then turned on her heel.

"Wait."

The woman paused.

"Why did you tell me that?" Sam asked.

"Slow as hell around here." She grinned. "Looks to me like you're here to stir things up."

Well, Sam told herself with a resigned sigh, there was no need pretending that she didn't stand out like flashing neon here in Monroeville. George had said that the tax auction was at eleven. She might as well blunder on in.

There didn't seem to be any other place to ask, so she checked in at the courthouse.

"Excuse me," she said to the secretary in the first office she came to. "Can you tell me where the tax auction's being held?"

"Tax auction?" The plump young woman with bright pink skin stared at her through purple-rimmed glasses. "I don't know nothing about no tax auction. Clotile?" she called.

From the other side of a partition came a disembodied voice. "What?"

"You know anything about a tax auction?"

"Nope. I sure don't."

"Do you know who might?" Sam asked the plump woman.

"No, ma'am." The purple-rimmed glasses winked at her. "I sure don't."

"I think Sheriff Dodd will probably be there."

"Oh! Well, why didn't you say so? Sheriff Dodd is back in his office. Out that door"—she pointed—"and back to the right."

"Then the tax auction's in his office?"

"Honey, I don't know nothing about no tax auction. I just know where Sheriff Dodd is at."

Sam followed the woman's directions and stepped into the sheriff's office. "Is this where the tax auction's being held?" she asked the young deputy at the front desk. He was cursing softly at the green screen of a computer.

"Damned thing was put here by the state to drive us crazy," he said, looking up at her. "I'm sorry, ma'am, what was it you said you wanted?"

"The tax auction."

He pushed his hat farther back on his head. He looked like he was about eighteen years old. "Sorry, I don't know about any tax auction."

"How about Sheriff Dodd?"

He broke into a grin. Eager to be of help, he pointed. "He's back there in his office, visiting with Mr. Saunders."

"They're having a meeting?"

"No ma'am, I don't think so. I think they're just visiting. Why don't you go back and knock on the door?"

Sam walked down the hall and paused outside the

door marked *Sheriff.* She was about to knock when from inside she heard someone say, "Well, you just whistling Dixie, boy, is what I think." The voice was a soft rumble that reminded her of melted caramel.

"Well, I wouldn't be so sure about that," a higher voice responded.

Behind her, Sam heard footsteps. She was about to get caught eavesdropping. She knocked quickly.

"Come on in," called the rumble, and she opened the door. "Why, hi there, ma'am," said a big, dark, handsome man. He pulled his boots down off his desk and stood. "What can we do for you?"

"We" included the other man in the room, who was of medium build, with slightly buck teeth, middle-parted hair, and horn-rimmed glasses. Jeb Saunders looked like he'd be more at home at Yale than in Monroeville.

Sam held out her hand and introduced herself. "Susan Sloan. I'm looking for the tax auction."

"Well," Buford Dodd said, grinning, "you come to the right place, but you got the wrong time. Just missed it. It was over about five minutes ago. Have a seat." He pulled out a chair for her.

"Right here?" she asked, sitting down.

"Yep. Right here in this office."

"Where's everybody else?"

"Well, they've done gone."

Sam knew that Dodd was fooling with her. There had been nobody else in this room. Dodd, acting as tax commissioner, had just sold to himself, through the auspices of Jeb Saunders, some land that would eventually pass into the hands of Edison Kay or someone else who wasn't shy about stealing from people who couldn't pay their taxes.

"I'm looking for some land up here. What sold today?" she asked.

"Well, a couple of nice parcels." Saunders had one of those genteel Southern voices that always made Sam feel like she should go back to finishing school.

"Ten cents on the dollar?"

"Depends on what you thought the dollar value was in the first place." Saunders smiled.

They could go on like this all day. She was no match for these men, no match for anyone in Monroeville, for that matter. Though they might be friendly on the surface, they had more practice, *generations* of practice, at closemouthed horse-trading. She might as well go on home and figure out another approach.

"Well, I've got to be going," Saunders said, moving toward the door.

"Me, too." Sam stood.

"Hold up there, Miz Sloan," said Dodd. "It's not often we get visitors from the big city. Why don't you sit and visit for a while?"

That was more like it. "Why, thanks." She put her bag back down. "I'd be happy to."

"Now, what's a pretty lady like you doing up here alone looking for a tax auction?" Buford Dodd smiled. And then he stood up again, showing off his powerful body. His brown twill uniform fit as if it had been custom-tailored to his broad shoulders, his muscular thighs. He walked over to the open door and shut it firmly. "Coffee?"

Sam nodded.

"Sugar?" When he said the word, it sounded like its taste. He rolled it around on his tongue.

He brushed his hand against hers as he gave her the cup and was in no hurry to remove it. She was suddenly aware of being alone in the room with this man. She wondered if he'd locked the door when he closed it.

"Your husband too busy to make the trip?" He glanced pointedly at her unadorned left hand.

"The land will be in my name."

But he was as tenacious as a well-trained coon dog. "Then you *are* married?"

"Yes," she lied.

"I'm not." He grinned.

Two could play that game. Sam looked openly at the wide gold band on his left hand.

"My wife is," he said, and laughed.

Sam smiled only with the corners of her mouth and sipped her coffee. "So, do large parcels frequently come up for sale up here? My husband thinks that this is *the* county in which to buy. This and Pickens. He says values are going to be skyrocketing any day now, what with Atlanta growing so."

"Could be," Dodd said, sitting down on the edge of his desk, leaning just a little too close. "Course, we country boys wouldn't know. We just hunt and fish. Leave the fancy work to the lawyers and real estate developers."

It was the opening she'd been hoping for. "Speaking of lawyers, isn't this the area where that lawyer, Forrest Ridley, was found?"

"Not far from here. On up the road a piece."

"Appalachian Falls?"

"Apalachee. Guess you never been up there. You know Forrest Ridley?"

"No." She shook her head. "My husband does. But I read about it in the paper. Must have been awful, to die like that."

"I reckon after the first good lick on the head, you don't know what's happening. He looked like he took a few good ones."

"You saw the body? Oh, I guess you would have."

"Yep. We took him out of the water. Terrible accident. Brought him right in here." He pointed toward a back room. "Not anything a lady like you ought to be thinking about. Ugly sight."

Sam thought about Hoke's line—the corpses, pieces of corpses, mushy things that *used* to be corpses that she'd seen. She remembered the body of a young San Francisco woman who had been a sculptor, until a maniac with an artistry of his own had cut out her heart with a very sharp knife. She'd seen several examples of that man's handiwork, as carefully executed as if he were working on a series for a show.

"Yes," she said. "But I would like to see the falls. I hear they're quite pretty."

"Beautiful." He reached over and laid a massive hand on her arm. She didn't think she'd ever seen such a big hand. "I'm headed up that way today. Why don't you let me drive you?"

"Oh, no. I couldn't." Though she wanted to talk with Dodd further, she knew that she didn't want to be alone with him in a car for a second.

"Why not?"

"I have my dog." She gestured in the direction where she was parked.

"I like dogs. Raise bulldogs myself."

"Actually, I'm not coming back this way. I'm going to drive over into Pickens County. Thanks anyway."

"More land you're interested in over there?"

"Yes, near Tate." She stood.

"Well, if you're ever up here again," he said,

squeezing her arm, "I hope you'll come by and say hidey."

"Why, thank you. And thank you for the coffee." She smiled back at him. "You needn't show me out. Thanks for the hospitality, Sheriff Dodd."

Dodd stood watching out his window as she opened her car door and took the excited little white dog into her arms. Then he called back behind his shoulder to the deputy who had earlier made the joke about the dog being Chinese.

"You make her, Early?"

"Yep. Frank and I just got the goddamned computer to work. Samantha Adams. Reporter. *Atlanta Journal-Constitution.* Car's in her name."

"Married?"

"Single."

"Bitch." When Buford Dodd squinted as he was doing now, he looked very scary. He hitched up his gunbelt. "I thought so."

Fourteen

$\blacklozenge$

SAM HAD BEEN AWAKE SINCE HARPO HAD PADDED IN at six-thirty and gently leaned his front paws against the bed. Lying there staring out at the trees for a half hour, she'd been thinking about how creepy it had felt, standing up at the top of Apalachee Falls. She was trying to imagine what Forrest Ridley's last moments had been like. She tried the scenario first in the daytime, then at night. The latter was infinitely more terrifying.

She grabbed the phone on its first ring.

"What?" she asked.

"What? What kind of greeting is *what?"*

"The kind of greeting that someone deserves who has the gall to call someone at"—she reached for the clock and peered at it—"seven o'clock in the morning. This is a nasty habit you've developed."

"You've already been up for a while," he said.

"How do *you* know?"

"I saw you get up and go into the bathroom."

"What!"

169

"Remember that old telescope I used to have up here in my room? Mom has preserved everything. It's like a monument to my youth."

"I'm reporting you to the AMA!"

"You're still looking good, Sammy." He laughed. "Still looking *very* good."

"Swine!" She pulled the sheet up over her naked body, then wrapped the top sheet around her like a toga, stepped over to the window, and pulled the long curtains. Then she went back to the phone.

"Boo!" Beau said. "Hiss! Boo!"

"What do you want, anyway?"

"God," he sighed, "don't ask me that."

"I'm hanging up."

"Wait! We've got thousands of prints."

She said nothing.

"From the Virginia Circle house."

Nothing.

"A few of them yours."

Zero.

"The remainder belong to . . . are you ready?"

Zilch.

"Forrest Ridley and Totsie Kay."

"Hot damn! How do you know?"

"Well, Ridley's we were expecting, of course, but Totsie's we traced with the computer. She'd been printed because she's press."

"Of course. Totsie Kay. Jesus! He's old enough to be her father. And besides which . . ."

"Yep. Good clean prints throughout the house. In the bathroom. On the sheets."

"You printed the sheets?"

"Sure. Comes in real handy in rape cases. But I doubt very seriously that Ridley was raping her."

"Jeest! Totsie Kay. I can't get over it. She's friends with his daughter. He knew her when she was a little girl—he knew her parents before she was born." Sam paused. "So what does this mean? You think Queen found out and pushed him off the falls? Does that make sense?"

"Beats me. You're the dick."

"Let me remind you that I am not a private investigator. I am an investigative reporter, and you, my good Dr. Talbot, are a Peeping Tom."

"I thought you'd forgive me when I gave you the news."

"What about the surprise party note?"

"Nothing yet. We're still working on it."

"Then get back to work."

The second phone call came fifteen minutes later. It was from Cutting, Sam's San Francisco tracker.

"Campton Place," he said. "The man liked to eat well in the restaurant downstairs. The name of his very young, very blond lady friend was Totsie Kay. She didn't register that way, of course."

"Thanks," said Sam. "You're a quarter of an hour late."

"And twenty years too old and one hundred pounds too fat. You going to hold all that against me, Cookie-face?"

"Love you, Cutting," she said, and signed off.

"I stopped by last night," Liza was saying, "to have dinner with Queen. When I came in, she was yelling at someone on the phone."

"And?" asked Sam. She had waited until after

171

breakfast to check in with Ridley's daughter, which she did almost every day.

"It sounded just like a fight with my father. 'I don't want you to be late,' she said. 'I want you there. Now.'"

"Any ideas?"

"Nope. Lona doesn't know either. She said no men have come to the house. Just telephone calls. Though she said sometimes when she leaves, in the early evening, Queen is getting all dressed up to go out." She hesitated. "What's up, Sam?"

Sam put her off with a noncommittal answer. She wasn't going to tell Liza that her beloved father had been having an affair with one of her friends. She knew Liza didn't want to hear that. Though sooner rather than later, she was going to hear that and more—Sam felt it in her bones.

"Sure, I can meet you," said Totsie. "But weren't you coming over this evening to my parents' house? Dad said you wanted us all to be there to talk about Forrest Ridley."

"I did. I do. But there are a couple of things I'd like to talk to you about. Is right after work okay for you? Let's say, Walter Mitty's about six?"

"Sure," Totsie said, though she sounded a little uncertain. "Then we can go from there to the house."

Mitty's was filled with prosperous young Atlantans drinking Perrier and white wine, though Sam noticed that vodka seemed to be once again on the rise. The crowd fit all the stereotypes and acronyms: yuppies, dinks, sinks, and preppies. Someone once had told her that Atlanta was the Lacoste capital of the world, and this afternoon she believed it. On one young man she'd spied four visible alligators, and she'd bet good money that if she could get a look at his underwear, he'd total an even half-dozen.

Totsie hesitated in the doorway, frowning around the crowded room. What a pretty girl, Sam thought. No wonder Forrest Ridley was tempted. She waved, and Totsie flashed her smile, glittering white.

"So," Totsie asked even before settling her rear into the chair. "What did you want to know?"

"Whoa. Going to a fire? Let's order you a drink first. You look like you could use one." Sam flagged down the waiter. "Long day?" She turned back to Totsie, leaned a little closer, and took a deep breath. She thought she smelled the remnants of this morning's Chanel No. 5.

"They're all long when you first start, aren't they? I mean, it's slowly beginning to dawn on me that it's the people who make all the money who jet off to Paris. It's the young grinds like me who stay home and do the work."

Sam laughed. "Paying your dues, I think it's called. Learning the ropes."

They talked about television newscasting for a while, small talk, chitchat.

"So," Totsie repeated after her vodka and tonic arrived from the bar, "what did you want to know?" The young woman was obviously in a hurry to get this conversation on the road.

Sam led her gently, just as she'd planned, keeping it all nice and easy. She got Totsie to talk about growing up with Liza Ridley, the summers at Tate, the overnights at Lake Lanier, what it was like to be Simmons & Lee tykes.

"I don't quite understand," Totsie said finally, when Sam had picked up the check and they were walking out the door. "I thought you wanted to talk with me about Forrest. Aren't you doing a profile on Forrest Ridley? That's what Daddy said."

"Well, this is all background, you know. Oh." Sam struck herself lightly on the forehead. "I almost forgot. I found some old pictures that I thought I'd like to use, and I wanted you to help me identify the people in them, but I left them in my car. Do you mind walking to it?"

"Of course not."

"I'm afraid it's a little way away. I couldn't find a parking place. This neighborhood has really become something, hasn't it? It's better than it ever was when I was growing up."

Then Sam began chatting about famous people she'd met in her travels. When she dropped the name of Jane Pauley, she thought Totsie was going to faint.

On and on she went about Pauley, which wasn't hard because Totsie had a million questions—which was exactly what Sam had counted on when she'd planned this little stroll. The younger woman was so engrossed that she lost all her earlier hesitation and, more importantly, didn't pay any attention to where they were going. They'd turned right off Greenwood onto Barnett, and in just a few more steps they'd be on Virginia Circle. Two doors up was Totsie and Forrest Ridley's secret pied-à-terre. One door. Zero.

"Here we are," Sam announced.

Totsie looked at her, glanced at the car, then stared beyond it at the house. One hand fluttered to her mouth like a loopy white butterfly.

Sam took a deep breath and closed the net. "You want to tell me about it?"

They sat together in the car. Totsie talked and cried, and Sam listened and handed her tissues.

"It happened, I don't know how. He is—*was*—old enough to be my father. But he was a wonderful man." She turned to Sam with eyes pleading for understanding. "He was really someone special."

Sam nodded.

"I know what we were doing was wrong. But he was so miserable at home . . . and when we were together, it didn't seem wrong. Do you know what I mean?"

God, who didn't? But when they were Totsie's age, they thought they'd invented it all—sex, drugs, temptation. Each generation thinks it invented the whole ball of wax.

"We talked about everything. We shared everything. We were perfect together." A freshet poured down her face, and with it went the last of her mascara.

Sam decided to take a flier. "Did you share with Forrest your knowledge of your father's land deals up in Watkin County?" she asked.

Totsie jerked back as if she'd been slapped.

"I guess the answer's yes," Sam said, then pushed onward, hoping she was on a roll. "Did you tell your father that you'd told Ridley?"

"Of course not!"

"Your father doesn't know about your relationship with Forrest Ridley?"

"No. It would kill him," Totsie choked out.

"It must have been very complicated for you, your

father and Forrest being old friends and partners and all. What did Forrest say when you told him about your father using your name on deeds?"

"He was very upset. He . . . oh, it was just awful. All of a sudden he was investigating Daddy's dealings inside the firm. He said he thought Daddy'd been up to something, that he was using it as shelter, to launder funds."

"Was there *that* much money?"

Totsie grew very quiet. Sam looked closely to see if she was still breathing.

"Forrest said there was millions. That there was something going on even more than land." Once again her voice rose. "It was terrible! If only I'd kept my big mouth shut. Everything was so wonderful between us for a while. We had great times together. We took trips. We . . ." She gestured at the little house, and her voice broke. "Then I ruined it all. Forrest was obsessed with finding out what was going on up in Monroeville. With *my* daddy!" She fumbled at the car door. Suddenly it had all become too much for her. "Let me out. I want to go home!"

"You're too upset to drive. I'll take you."

"No! I can drive myself."

"Are you sure?"

"Yes!" Totsie took a deep breath, chest out. "I can take care of myself."

Sam doubted that. But on second thought, maybe she could. Totsie was an interesting combination of peaches and steel.

"Okay," Sam agreed. But she wasn't letting Totsie out of her sight. "I'll take you to your car. Then I'll follow you."

Totsie wheeled. "Why? Haven't we talked enough?"

"We have a date with your parents. Have you forgotten?"

"You're going to tell them, aren't you?" Once again she was a little girl.

"I'm not going to tell them anything."

"Not your job to snitch?"

"No."

"That's all this is to you, isn't it? A job? A story?" Totsie's spunk was back.

"No. No more than it would be only that for you if you were doing it for television. I really want to find out what happened to Forrest Ridley. Don't you?"

Beside her, Totsie leaned her pretty head back against the leather upholstery and moaned.

Fifteen

◆

IN THAT CASE, CAN WE CHANGE OUR PLANS A BIT?"
Edison Kay spoke softly into the telephone in his
library. "Instead of the usual place, why don't you
stop by here for a drink? She'll be here any minute."

"Yes!" He laughed at the response on the other end
of the line. "Me, too! Can't wait to see her. But let's
save it for a while. This is rude, but why don't you
bring your own bottle and sit in your car around back
for a while? I think if you're patient, we'll find
something to amuse you."

"Well, it's awfully good to see y'all." Kay Kay gave
Totsie a hug, then extended her hand, missing Sam's
by just a hair. The fading Texas beauty was already
drunk. "Come on in and have a little tiddly. Edison
will be with us in just a moment."

Totsie stepped toward the sideboard in the sitting
room. Crystal decanters with little silver name tags
littered its top. "Don't mind if I do, Mama," she said,
her hand on the vodka. "Sam?"

"Perrier or soda water."

"You *are* a party-pooper," Kay Kay said, slurring a little, "aren't you?"

"Had to give up the drinking." Sam smiled, but inside she wondered, as she had frequently in the years she'd been sober, how many times she had made a fool of herself in public, been a sloppy drunk just like Kay Kay. "But not the good times," she finished.

"Don't know how you think you can have a party without a little drink." Kay Kay turned as her husband entered the room. "Isn't that so, Edison?"

"Whatever you say, dear."

It was a condescending smile, thought Sam, that reeked of smug self-assurance. It was a smile that she had seen all her life on the faces of certain men who thought they pulled all the strings, thought that they had those strings wrapped around a finger in their pocket, that all they had to do was crook that finger and you'd jump because that string was tied to you.

"Samantha." He pulled her to his shirtfront in a big hug of assumed familiarity. "So good to see you. How are you doing?"

"Fine." She leaned back and said into his face, "It's good of you to give me the time tonight. I won't take long. Don't want to keep you from your dinner."

He relaxed his hold on her. "Oh, we eat late—when we eat." And he smiled that oily smile again at Kay Kay, who lifted her drink to him in salute. "We're glad to do it. Anything for the memory of Forrest. Isn't that right, dear?"

He turned to Totsie and gave her a hug, too. "How you doing, baby? Haven't seen you in a couple of days. You're looking a little peaked."

"I'm fine, Daddy." She pulled herself straight, shoulders back like a little soldier.

"Well," he said, gesturing, "shall we sit?"

Sam led them through an easy ramble first, just as she had done with Totsie earlier. Drawing them out was an easy task because for most Southerners, storytelling is as natural as breathing. Up and down the rhythms flew; she needed only a light touch on the reins to keep them going in the right direction.

Though Edison took center stage, from time to time Kay Kay chimed in, adding a detail. Totsie was quiet, a small smile fixed in place. She looked like any dutiful Southern wife at a dinner party. Considering her earlier conversation with Sam in front of the love nest, it was a masterful display of self-control.

And throughout the talk, the liquor flowed. Before long, three decanters sat on the coffee table before them. Bourbon for Edison, vodka for Totsie. Kay Kay drank gin.

An hour passed, then two. Sam knew that good manners called for her to leave and let these people eat their dinner. But politeness wasn't her goal.

Edison was just finishing a story about Forrest chartering a bus to take a group of friends down to Auburn for a football game. "He went to Georgia, you know, undergrad, and was a rabid Bulldogs fan. He insisted that we all come along. Picked up the whole tab. Had the trip catered, too—champagne all the way. First class."

"He was a very generous man," Totsie murmured.

"And a great practical joker," Kay Kay said, reaching for her gin. She was drinking it neat now.

"Really?" Sam asked. "I didn't know that."

"Oh, yes." Kay Kay waved a hand in an extravagant gesture. "Not so much in the last few years, but he pulled off some lulus in his time."

"Go on," Sam encouraged.

"Don't you remember, Edison," she asked, "that time we got such terrible service in that awful Italian restaurant on Piedmont—Gallo's, was that it?"

"Yes," Edison said, chuckling. "Gallo's. They went out of business."

"And Forrest helped them along. He went back that next Saturday afternoon dressed like a Georgia Power man and turned off their electricity. Right when they were getting ready for a huge wedding party. It was wonderful."

Kay Kay laughed. Then for a moment there was only the tinkle of crystal and ice in the room. Sam waited.

"Oh, and remember?" Kay Kay went on as the gin lubricated her reminiscences. "That story he told us about when he was in school at Virginia, in law school. And he had this professor he didn't like?"

"I don't recall this one."

"Well, maybe you weren't there when he told it. That's right," she gushed, patting Edison's knee and sloshing a little gin on his trousers. "Oh, I'm sorry, dear. I think you were away on business, and Forrest and Queen were over for drinks. Are you *sure* you never heard it?"

"No. Go on." Edison's voice was impatient, but Kay Kay didn't notice.

"Anyway, he told this hilarious story about this *awful* professor he had. Everybody simply detested the man. And what Forrest did was, he waited until almost the end of the term, kissy-facing up to the man the whole time, and then he went to a printer in some little town in Virginia, away from Richmond."

"Charlottesville," said Edison.

"I thought you never heard this story." Kay Kay turned to her husband, slopping a little more gin.

"Jesus, Kay Kay. Be more careful." Edison stood, wiping at his arm with a cocktail napkin.

"Well, how do you know it wasn't Richmond?" she insisted.

"Because UVA is in Charlottesville."

"Oh." Kay Kay sat for a moment digesting that fact, her face as placid as a cow's.

"So what happened?" asked Sam, who'd gotten a tingling in her toes when Kay Kay mentioned the printer. She thought she knew where this story was headed.

"Well, he went to this printer outside of *Charlottesville,* and he got him to print up hundreds of invitations to a party at this professor's house. And he sent them to all the faculty and all the law students, but he didn't send one to the professor. So this professor and his wife were sitting around one evening, watching TV or whatever, when all these hundreds of people showed up."

Kay Kay sat back in her seat with a triumphant grin on her face. The room was silent.

"Don't you think that's funny?" she continued when no one spoke. "I mean, don't you get it, that all these people were there for a party, and the professor didn't have anything but a six-pack, maybe, and some peanuts? I thought it was the funniest thing I ever heard. I'll never forget it. I'd love to do that to somebody sometime."

Then she popped her hand to her mouth like a naughty child who's spilled the beans.

And you did, didn't you? Sam thought in the deepening silence. She glanced at Edison Kay. He gave her an even, curtained look in return.

You crafty son-of-a-bitch, she thought. Poker players, you lawyers, all of you. You know that I know that Kay Kay sent those invitations. But *why?* Why was she punishing Ridley? Because she knew her daughter was having an affair with him? You knew that, too, didn't you? You know everything. You *do* hold all the strings.

"Well, it's getting a little late." Edison stood. "Maybe we ought to finish this up another time, Samantha."

"I still don't know why nobody thinks that's funny," Kay Kay complained.

"Because it's not, Mother." Totsie's voice was on the edge.

"Please don't bother. I can find my way out," Sam said, and hurriedly stepped into the hallway outside the room. She didn't want to let Edison usher her out the front door. Not just yet, for she could feel something coming. She stood stock still in the hall, listening. This was about to get very good.

"You're drunk, Mother. Why don't you go to bed?"

"Listen, little lady." Kay Kay was getting her Texas up. She pointed a finger in Totsie's face. "Don't you tell your mother what to do. I was drinking before you were born."

"Obviously. You've been drunk my whole life."

"Honey, honey, calm down." Edison put his arm around his daughter. "What's all this to-do? Come on, sugar. Spend the night here with us. Go upstairs to

183

your old room. Goodness," he said, brushing Totsie's blond hair back from her forehead, "I didn't think this talk about Forrest was going to get everyone so upset."

"Oh, Daddy," Totsie wailed, as if she were twelve years old. "I miss him so."

The vodka had caught up with her. The vodka and the grief.

"Well, well." He patted her on the back. "We all do. Forrest was such a good friend to us all."

"Yes, wasn't he?" Kay Kay added, seeming to focus more clearly than she had in the past hour. "He and Queen. Such good friends to us all."

Edison shot Kay Kay a warning look.

"He was my best friend," Totsie continued. "Oh, Daddy, I loved him so."

"I know, pumpkin. We all did."

Sam stepped back into the room. "I'm sorry, I'm afraid I forgot my . . ." She let her words trail off, but Totsie, as she'd hoped, kept going.

"But not like I did," the girl wailed, as if it were suddenly important that she differentiate *her* love, *her* grief from theirs, that she get the sympathy that was her just due, no matter what its cost. "He was *my* lover."

Kay Kay dropped her glass. It thudded on the heavy carpet, and the gin spread in a darkening circle.

"You knew that, you bastard," Kay Kay snarled at her husband. "You knew that all the time, didn't you?" Then she lunged toward him with one arm drawn back.

Edison grabbed her wrist. "Hush now, Kay Kay. You're upset. You're drunk."

"You're goddamned right I'm upset! Did you give

184

Forrest your daughter, Edison? Did you give him her body in exchange for his silence? You'd do anything, wouldn't you, anything, to keep the money flowing— that pipeline of money that fuels your dick. Isn't that what makes you hard, Ed? I know *I* haven't for years. But money does, doesn't it? Money does the trick."

"No!" Totsie screamed. "Shut up!"

Edison turned as if suddenly realizing that Sam was still in the room. "You'll have to excuse us, Samantha. My girls seem to be a little hysterical tonight."

Sam smiled and stood her ground.

Edison didn't return the smile. "I hate to be rude, but . . ." He didn't finish the sentence. Men like him didn't have to. They were used to people moving out of their way at the slightest innuendo.

"You hate to be rude!" Totsie shrieked. "All this goddamned standing on ceremony. Forrest's dead and buried, and we all walk around pretending that we're at a tea party!"

"Come on," Kay Kay said tiredly, as if she'd been deflated. "Let's go to bed, Totsie."

But Totsie was hardly ready for bed. "That's all anyone ever does in this goddamned house! In this goddamned town! Just sit around being polite and telling amusing stories until something ugly comes up, something unpleasant, something like real life, and then suddenly everybody excuses themselves from the room. 'Pardon me,' they say, 'I've got to check on something.' Or, 'I'm so tired. I have to go to bed.' Well, check on this. I killed Forrest!"

"Totsie, no!" Kay Kay screamed.

"What are you talking about, child?" Edison had the most peculiar look on his face.

"I killed him! I did it!" Totsie was hysterical, totally

out of control. "We came back from San Francisco, though Forrest pretended that he was still there, still gone. And I drove up to the falls with him. We went in separate cars. We took a little cabin up there, at the base of Apalachee."

Sam remembered seeing the cabins there, up above the campgrounds.

"Forrest said that he had some business he needed to take care of. With *you*, Daddy." She whirled and pointed her finger at him. "With you and Sheriff Dodd. He said he wanted to tell you that he knew what was going on with the land deals, and the money, and that you had to stop." Totsie's breathing was ragged.

Edison shrugged. "It was nothing, honey. Just bending conventions a little among old friends. I've known Buford Dodd for a long time."

"And Jeb Saunders?" Totsie flung the name at him like a weapon.

"Yes, dear." His voice was soothing, as if he were talking to an upset child. "Jeb's an associate of the firm. We do a lot of business together."

"Shut up!" Kay Kay spat the words in her husband's face. "Shut up! I know what you're doing. You always do it! You're twisting this to be what you want. Well, it's not. It's not what you want at all. Totsie's talking about killing Forrest Ridley. Do you understand that?" Veins stood out in her neck; her eyes protruded.

Totsie raced on as if she couldn't stop. "When he came back to the cabin after seeing you all, he was upset. He said that he had found proof of lots more money that you all had hidden, that you were going to ruin the firm, and that he had to turn you in.

"But *you* said, he said *you* said that he couldn't do that. That *it* would ruin the firm and my good name. He said *you* said that Mama and I would never be able to hold our heads up in the Driving Club again. That we'd be banned. As if that mattered." Her laughter was manic.

"I told him that, I told him I didn't care. All I wanted was for us to be like we used to before I told him about your crooked deals. Why did I ever tell him?" She cradled her wet face in splayed fingers. "If I hadn't, he'd be alive now."

"Totsie, Totsie," her mother crooned, hugging herself with her arms. "It's not your fault. What these men do is never our fault."

"It *is*, Mama. You don't understand. He said that he was going to have to think it all over. That it was probably a good idea if we stopped seeing one another until all this was worked out.

"'No!' I screamed. I was crazy. I couldn't stand the idea that he was going to leave me. I've never been so happy, never before in my life. I was crying and pulling on his clothes. I was on my knees begging, 'No, Forrest, no.'

"'Baby,' he said, 'you don't understand. This is wrong. It's all wrong. I have to think this over.'

"And then something snapped inside me. It was like something broke. I just didn't care anymore. If I couldn't have Forrest, I couldn't—I couldn't go on."

"Sugar, sugar," Kay Kay moaned, partly for her daughter and partly for herself. "Oh, Jesus, look where they push you. Right to the brink. And over."

"I ran out the door to my car," Totsie said. "But I'd left my keys inside. Then I grabbed my gun from the glove compartment."

"Oh, Totsie." Kay Kay's eyes were wide, like those of a frightened horse.

"I ran out into the dark. I ran faster and faster, I didn't really know where I was going. I just kept running. I could hear Forrest behind me. He was calling for me to stop. But I kept running, up, up. 'I'll kill myself when I get to the top,' I kept whispering to myself. 'When I get to the top.' Then I wouldn't have this terrible pain inside. It would all be over. It *was* already over, don't you understand? If I couldn't have Forrest, I was already dead."

"Oh, honey," Kay Kay crooned. "How could you think that?"

It's easy, Sam thought, don't you know that? Hanging in there with Edison all these years? Isn't desertion your greatest fear, Kay Kay? Being alone?

Sam turned and looked at Edison. He was standing completely still, like a stone statue in a rainstorm. It was all washing over him. All just words. He was merely waiting for the facts beneath the emotions, the facts that might relate to him, the facts that might cost him money or power, the important things.

Totsie raced on. "So I kept running and running. A couple of times I fell, and I was afraid that he was going to catch me and stop me. But"—and she smiled then, a wonderful ruined smile that Sam didn't want to look at too long because she felt it might break your heart—"Forrest wasn't really much of an athlete. The most exercise he ever got was the walks over to our house on Virginia Circle." She turned to Sam, who nodded.

"What house?" Kay Kay demanded.

Totsie shook her head. It wasn't important now.

She pushed on. "And finally I *was* at the top, at the top of the path, the top of the falls. I stood there, holding the gun in my hand, listening to the rush of all that water. Before it comes to the falls it's very quiet, you know. It's really just a little stream, but it grows as it falls over, and then it bounces, it spews, it foams. Of course, I couldn't see any of that in the darkness. I could only *hear* it down below. I stood there, Mama, thinking how glad I was that you taught me to shoot when I was a little girl, and that you'd always insisted that I keep a gun in my car for protection. And then I turned the gun toward my head."

"Oh, Totsie." Kay Kay was sobbing.

"But I'd waited too long, listening to the falls. Forrest ran up behind me. He grabbed me. And then the gun went off. There was a report, and he jolted. We had our arms around each other. And then he fell." She looked at Sam as if Sam could make some sense out of this tale she was telling that didn't make any sense to her, even though she'd been there. "He fell over the rail, over the falls. I couldn't even scream. I just stood there, like it was a joke. Like it was a video that any moment I could reverse, and he would come back up the falls, over the rail, and I would hold him again in my arms. Then I would push the stop button, and that would be the end. There wouldn't be any gunshot. We would stand there at the top of the falls in the dark, and he would whisper in my ear, 'I love you, baby,' and then we'd go to bed." She whispered, "Just like that."

Totsie stood with her arms open in a circle. Her mother walked into the circle and enveloped her.

Edison turned. His face was somber. "Well, Samantha. You can see that this was all a tragic accident." He placed an arm around her shoulders and, this time, propelled her toward the front door.

"Terribly tragic," he went on. "I hope we'll talk about this tomorrow before you share this story with anyone."

He managed to pat her, but at the same time he was still politely walking her out. "And now, if you'll excuse us, it's been a long night. I must put my pretty ladies to bed."

The door clicked behind her suddenly, and before she knew what was happening, Sam was standing alone in the dark.

Sixteen

◆

SAM SHOOK HER HEAD AS SHE WHEELED HER CAR DOWN the long driveway. So Totsie had accidentally killed Ridley. And then what? Did she just leave his body there to be discovered and wait for the announcement of his death, which came, ironically enough, at her parents' cocktail party?

Why would she do that? Because she was afraid she'd be charged with murder? Or because she didn't want anyone to know about the circumstances?

Or was it simply fear? Had she just panicked? Sam thought about Chappaquiddick. She'd always wondered what she'd do in a situation like that, a fatal accident, but a terribly incriminating one. It was easy to condemn others until you were standing there, looking at a dead body, trying to make a rational *and* moral decision while you were in shock.

But something about Totsie's story bothered her. It wasn't that Sam didn't believe her. She believed that Totsie *thought* that was the way it had happened. Sam couldn't quite put her finger on it, but it didn't feel quite right.

Maybe it was Edison's reaction to Totsie's story. He didn't really seem concerned about her, but rather, curious about what she was going to say. And his being in the vicinity of the accident, even ten miles away—somehow it was like being ten miles away from an atomic bomb.

Sam stopped at the end of the drive, turned left on Andrews, then left on West Paces Ferry Road. She'd take I-75 back home. Though she usually avoided the expressways, she was in a hurry. She wanted to talk to George about all this. And to Beau. In light of Totsie's story, she wanted to talk with him again about that hole he thought he'd seen in Ridley's chest—and to tell him to check the note for Kay Kay's fingerprints.

So Kay Kay had sent those invitations. What else was she capable of doing? Was she capable of murder? And why had she pulled that stunt? It would be a long reach to think a woman her age would go to so much trouble for a practical joke. Why did she dislike the Ridleys so? Or *one* of the Ridleys? Was it Forrest or Queen?

What was it she'd said about Queen at Forrest's wake? Something about Queen coming after other women's husbands. Was Queen after *her* husband? It had sounded tonight as if the Kays' match had hardly been made in heaven, as if the love had gone long ago. But who knew why people stayed together, why they held on, the dependencies and needs they fed for one another? Edison Kay might be a son-of-a-bitch, but he was *Kay Kay's* son-of-a-bitch, and rich to boot.

On the other hand, why would Queen be interested in Edison Kay? Maybe she knew about Ridley's affair with Totsie. Maybe this was her little joke—keeping it all in the family, so to speak. All that plastic surgery . . . and yet Forrest was seeing a young girl. Was that all a—

Sam's heart dropped. There was a blue light, damn it, rotating in her rearview mirror.

She jerked her foot off the gas and looked down at the needle. Shit! She'd been doing fifty-five. The speed limit in this neighborhood was probably forty. Should she tell this guy some cock and bull story about being on assignment? Hell, it was worth a try.

She slowed and edged the car off the pavement. The patrol car pulled up right behind her.

She reached into her bag for her driver's license, registration, and her press card. Though you could never tell with these guys—some of them hated the media. She'd decide when she saw him how to play it.

"Sorry, ma'am, but I'm going to have to ask you to get out of the car."

"Just a minute." Sam glanced to her left, but his flashlight was blinding. "If you'll hold that still a second, I'll have my license."

"Please, just step out of the car."

As he spoke the second time, the voice started to register. Low and rumbling, but pleasant. Beneath the rumble, just below the slow, sweet surface, was a chuckle. She'd heard that voice before. Yesterday? No, the day—

Just as she got it, Sheriff Buford Dodd, who'd been parked in the Kays' driveway nursing a bottle all during Sam's interview, grabbed her arm and jerked her out the door.

Seventeen

◆

THE HANDCUFFS SNAPPED. THE DOORLOCKS POPPED shut. The car began to move.

"Well now, *Mrs. Sloan*," Dodd drawled. In the flash of his nickel-plated lighter she saw his smile. He lit a cigar. "I hope you don't mind if I smoke."

So that's how he was going to play it—gentlemanly and cool. As if he'd just happened to be in the neighborhood. As if he'd invited her for a ride in his car and she'd smilingly accepted, swishing her skirts and showing a bit of ankle as he held the door and handed her inside.

"Not at all. But I do mind these." She lifted her braceleted wrists.

"I'm sorry about that." He chuckled. "Unfortunately, we have to do that kind of thing with uppity women. Now, had you minded your own business, had you stayed home . . ." He took a long drag on his cigar, and the car filled with smoke.

They passed the governor's mansion on their right, an atrocious red-brick reproduction of a Southern

194

plantation house whose first occupant had been Lester Maddox, that baseball bat-wielding racist champion. Just ahead was the green sign for I-75. Dodd turned onto the expressway, headed north.

What was it that sweet loony, Herman Blanding, had said? Something about the devil coming from the north? He'd been talking about Union soldiers, dead these many long years. But there were always men who were willing to wreak havoc on the bodies and happiness of others, whether they were fighting for a cause or were only in it for themselves. There always had been. Probably always would be. These devils favored no direction. They came from everywhere.

"Mrs. Sloan. Now, that was right insulting, you know, thinking you could fool us country boys with a phony name. It's not like we just crawled out of the slime yesterday."

Sam was trying to remember the psychological strategies she had once learned in a self-defense class in California. The class had been taught by a cop—just like her captor. Should she go along with him? Should she smile and be nice? Or should she be tough?

She tried nice first. "I didn't mean to insult you. You know, reporters just use whatever they think will get them by."

"Well, that's all right." He reached over and patted her knee. Then he rested his huge hand there and squeezed, kneading her flesh. He shifted his hand just a little higher, and turned and winked at her.

Uh-oh. Was this to be a *real* abduction—with a full complement of horrors?

"Naw," he said as if he were talking to himself. He lifted his hand and twirled his cigar. Sam stared at him, trying to second-guess his next move. The rolling of the fat stogie in his wet mouth was an obscenity. He felt her looking and grinned.

"Don't you want to know where we're going?"

"Of course I do."

"Then ask me."

Sam was silent. What kind of game was he playing? And how should she respond? Should she join in and play along? Or should she stay outside, strong?

In the self-defense class, the officer had said that the best thing you could do was escape. Well, she didn't see how she could do that. If you couldn't, you had to play it by ear, moment by moment.

"I said, 'Ask me,'" he insisted, his voice growing rougher.

"Where are we going?"

"'Where are we going, *please?*'" His right hand grasped the back of her neck. His powerful fingers reached almost all the way around. Jesus. He could choke her to death with one hand while still driving.

"Where are we going, *please?*"

"Pretty please."

"Pretty please."

"I'm taking you home." He shook her as if she were a kitten, and then released her. "Home to Monroeville."

He didn't talk for a long while after that. They turned east onto the perimeter highway, then north on Route 400. He drove swiftly and surely, the heavy car whooshing up the black road. Of course nobody was going to give *him* a ticket. He fiddled with the radio a moment; then a country and western station clicked in on a clear signal. Kenny Rogers was singing one of

Sam's old favorites about a philandering woman named Lucille.

Suddenly, on a dark stretch of road, Dodd wheeled over to the shoulder and flipped on his whirling blue light.

He was going to kill her right here. Sam froze. He was going to kill her right here on the side of the road in plain view of the cars rushing past, without her ever even knowing the whole story. She was never going to know what had really happened at Apalachee Falls—or why.

You are a trooper, Adams. And something else—a fool. Fighting for that story to the very last. Well, look where it got you this time, Ms. Smartypants, in a world of trouble that you know nothing about. It's not as if they didn't warn you: George, Hoke, Peaches and Horace, the DEA agent. And Beau. Beau. She was never going to know what that was all about, either. What it *could* have been. What the hell Beau really wanted.

Dodd reached over and unlocked her right cuff. Before she had time to massage her wrist, he grasped her arm and twisted it up sharply behind her back. She cried out. He drew her against his chest, forced his mouth down on hers. She struggled against him, tasting the cigar and stale whiskey. Then she heard a click.

She froze.

He's pulled a switchblade.

He's cocked a pistol.

I'm dead, she thought.

Then he released her.

He'd crossed her wrists and fastened them behind

197

her back. He pulled the seat belt across her chest, brushing her breasts with his fingers, and fastened it. Click.

"I should have done that in the first place," he said, grinning.

Then from the glove compartment he pulled a brown envelope, poured out some powder on a small mirror, drew two lines, and snorted.

"Whoo-ee!" he shouted, the sound bouncing around in the car. "White line fever! You want some?"

She shook her head.

"Might as well," he said. "No need to worry now about getting addicted."

"No, thank you."

"Want to keep your wits about you, huh?"

Yes. That was it exactly.

"Might as well enjoy yourself, honey." He switched on the ignition, and the powerful engine roared in response. The car jumped forward. "Won't make a damn bit of difference."

The cocaine made him talkative. The words rushed out in gobs like blood from a wound that couldn't be stanched.

"Lots more where this comes from," he bragged. "Straight from the La Guajira Peninsula."

"Colombia?"

"Smart girl. You bet."

"So you have your own personal supplier?"

He tipped his head back and laughed. "Supplier? Sweet thing, I'm part of the conduit. Those old boys, daredevils, fly that stuff straight in. That's what you wanted to know when you were asking about airstrips in Millie's, wuddn't it?"

Sam blushed in the dark. Of course, he knew every word that was ever spoken in Monroeville. Especially the words of a stranger. How stupid she'd been. What the hell did she think she was doing? She'd never been so sloppy before. What had she been thinking about? Maybe it *was* time she quit this business. She was going to think about doing that very thing, if she got the chance.

"What made you think there was drugs?" he demanded.

"Everybody knows they're coming in up here. And the more I looked, the more there seemed to be too much money."

"What d'ya mean?"

"You and Edison Kay—and Saunders. Laundering too much money, I thought, for it just to be land deals."

"That bastard!" he growled.

"Kay?"

"Nawh. Though he's prob'ly one too. They all are. City sharps, think they putting it to us old boys. Always working a slicker angle. Nawh." He shook his head. "Saunders. Greedy bastard. Always whining about his share. Hell, he didn't do half the work I did. Grunt work, standing out there in the middle of the night with flashlights, those little suckers swooping in like kamikazes, miss and they take your head off. Two minutes on the ground. Hustling for those duffels they tossed. Sweating like a nigger, reeling 'em in before anybody comes, sacks weighing two hundred pounds. Two hundred pounds a bag," he repeated, "of pure snow. And all Saunders did was make a few contacts. Didn't ever see him hustling *his* butt."

"But he was fifty-fifty on the land deals?"

"Oh, yeah, he did his share on that. But that was all the deal behind the deals, don't you see? The land is one thing. And it ain't chicken feed. But the blow's where the real bucks are." He sniffed, rubbing the back of his hand across his nose.

"You mean the land deals were just a cover-up for the drugs?"

"Not a cover-up, not exactly. But they're a way for funneling the money, and they turn a healthy profit themselves."

"This was Saunders's idea?" Sam pressed.

"Hell, no. Saunders ain't got those kind of brains. It was Kay. Kay's the sharpy. Kay's the one. Course"— and he puffed up—"he couldn't do none of it without me. I'm the . . . facilitator."

Sam wondered where he'd gotten that word—from watching detectives on TV? Or did Chuck Norris use fancy words in the movies these days before he blasted people's faces off with tommy guns?

"I've got to have a little talk with Saunders," Dodd continued as if he were alone. "Got to set him straight on a few things, like snitching to the GBI."

Sam held her breath.

"Wasn't no need to call anyone about Ridley. Didn't need the fucking M.E. up here messing around in our bidness." He was talking about Beau.

"Well, he didn't see much, did he?" Sam said.

They had turned off on Route 19 some time ago. Only here and there showed a light in a mobile home, the blue glow of a television screen, people inside clustered around a little picture of people being abducted, tortured, raped, killed—just like in real life. In real life it didn't happen as often, Sam thought. But it only had to happen to you once.

"He only saw Ridley's body in my office," Dodd said. "That didn't tell him nothing, 'cept the man was dead. And we already knew that." He relighted his cigar, which had gone out. "That's okay. Hell, I like to watch those monkeys work. All that tromping around the crime scene, looking for little bits of blood and hair, teeth and spit. They're like catfish. Bottom feeders. Sucking up the shit everybody else has left behind. Hell, we don't *ever* need to bother with those bastards. What else do we pay a vet good money for?" He laughed.

Sam doubted that Beau would appreciate that description of his profession. Nor would Boggs. She smiled a little at the thought of that kind-faced man. There was steel behind that sweet exterior. Was Boggs a Clark Kent? Would he quick-change into Superman, like the father who wanted to save his daughter B.J. from marriage in the shaggy dog story? If Boggs knew what was going on right now, would he swoop right down and save her?

She didn't think of Beau as her rescuer, even though he had the Superman looks. But then, she couldn't trust Beau. When it came to the clutch, he might excuse himself with some more important responsibility, some more pressing engagement, just might remember he wanted to go off and marry someone else.

No, when she thought about him, she thought other things, private things, warm things, lustful things. Jesus. She was still a sucker for his pretty face. She closed her eyes and let her thoughts loose. The two of them were naked, their bodies interwined, his mouth slowly working its way lower and lower down her back. He was planting soft little kisses down her spine. The tingling raced up and down, but mostly down. He had wrapped a leg around her. Then his knee slid up between her legs. She ran her hands over him, touching whatever came within reach. She was playing his ribs, musical ribs. They sang to her. He slipped a hand between her legs now, and she started to sing, too.

"You know Doc Talbot?"

Sam jumped. "Yes."

"Handsome fellow, ain't he?"

She nodded.

"Say what?"

"Yes!"

"Yes, what?"

Uh-oh, here we go again. "Yes, he's handsome."

"Better-looking than me?"

"No. He's not better-looking than you."

"Then," he drawled, "if you think he's handsome, you must think I'm Robert Redford, right?"

She paused. Any idiot could see where this was leading.

"I think you're a very handsome man, Sheriff Dodd." And actually, that was the truth. He was also mean as a rattlesnake. And just as sidewinding. You could never tell exactly where he was going to strike.

"Then I guess that means you want to fuck me." He reached over and grasped her face with one hand, twisting it toward him. "Right?"

"Wrong."

"Well." He laughed and released her. "You'll be begging for it before it's over."

And then he dropped that topic as if it were a toy he'd grown bored with.

"Thought he was slick, asking me all those questions about Ridley," Dodd grumbled. "Asking me about that hole in his chest. Any jackass could see that it was a gunshot. But I told him Ridley's body must have hit a rock. And he had to buy it, no matter what he knew, 'cause I wasn't letting nobody autopsy the body. It was an accidental death. Because *I* said so. That's what counts in Watkin County."

They were banking around Long Pond Bend. In a minute or two, they'd be in town.

"Just like when Ridley came busting up here, like he was somebody, Mr. Big Shot, in his six-hundred-dollar suit, comes in my office and tells me and Kay he knows what's going on and we got to stop. Hell, he didn't know crap about what was going on! A little bit about the money flowing through his precious office, a little bit about Kay's wife and the girl's names on deeds. Hell, he didn't know nothing."

Dodd rolled down the window and spat out onto the highway.

"But he was trouble. If he kept squawking his mouth around, other people who could see beyond their noses would figure it out. So when I said to Kay, 'Let's kill him,' it was *my* decision that counted. *My* word. You understand?"

"Yes, I understand," Sam said softly.

Dodd grew more animated. They were driving right through the hamlet of Monroeville, around the old courthouse, past Millie's. The lights were out. Sam wondered for a moment what Millie did for amusement in a town like this. Dodd killed people. Saunders made money. But what did a red-haired midget waitress who was thirsting for excitement do? Did she take truck drivers home with her? Did she run into Atlanta to party? Or drive north, with other women's husbands, up toward Apalachee Falls?

That's where they were headed now.

"So when he stormed out of here," Dodd continued, "puffed up, full of himself as if he were a judge delivering a verdict and telling us we'd better shape up and fly right, better clean our acts up, we followed him. Jumped in this very car and followed him up to the falls. Hell, he never even spotted us. Never looked back.

"We parked a little way down. I was carrying my Magnum. We'd make it look like a break and entry in his cabin. Easy, in and out. But there were two cars. We peeked in the window, and there was the girl. All in an uproar. Crying and shouting.

"I looked back at Kay. See, I didn't know who she was.

"'Want to take her out, too?' I asked.

"'No!' he said. 'That's my daughter.'

"He didn't really seem upset about that. Had this funny smile on his face." The sheriff shrugged. "Maybe he knew what was going down all along.

"Anyway, we waited for just a couple of minutes, and the girl, Totsie, came flying out the door, reached in her car, and came up carrying a pistol. Then Ridley came chasing after her. They were headed straight up the path to the top of the falls.

"I motioned to Kay and we jumped back in the car. We were waiting for them at the top when they got there.

"The girl was in much better shape. Kay was slower, winded. She was doing some fool thing with the gun, like she was going to kill herself, but you could tell she didn't really want to, was just bluffing. But Ridley didn't know that. And then, when he stepped in to take the gun away from her, that's when I took my shot. He fell over the edge of the falls just like a sack of potatoes."

"And Totsie?"

"Well, I guess she thought she'd done it, didn't she? She went to pieces. Wailing and screaming like you never heard. Then she pulled herself together, ran back down the path, and drove off in her car."

"And you haven't seen her since?"

"No. Not until tonight, when you all drove up to her daddy's house."

Sam's blood chilled. That was then, the tale he'd just finished telling. And this was now. This was her turn.

They were about five miles north of Monroeville now. Suddenly Dodd swung off onto a narrow road. It was black, Labrador black, coal black, black as death.

"Where are we going?"

"Uh, uh, uh." He waggled a finger at her like a schoolteacher.

"Please," she added.

"I want you to meet some friends of mine," he said. "You like dogs, don't you?"

Dust rose from beneath the heavy tires. Beyond the high beams was nothing but more road. Then the headlights fell on a small house, its front porch sagging. Sam heard dogs barking. Their cries grew louder at the car's approach.

She twisted, trying for the hundredth time to edge her crossed hands to the doorlock.

"You're just going to hurt yourself," Dodd said

without even turning his head to look at her. "You can't unlock it anyways. I have the controls. Just be patient." He pulled the car under a big tree and turned off the engine. "I'll get you out in just a second." He got out of the car.

"Hee-ah, boys!" he called to the barking dogs, who keened even higher at their master's voice.

Then he walked around the front of the car and opened Sam's door. He pulled her out, balancing her by her shoulders, then grasped the back of her neck and pushed her forward.

"They're going to know," she warned him, giving over all thought of trying to cajole him.

"Know what, missy?" he said, chuckling. "There ain't going to be much left to know when the dogs get through." He pushed her right up to the edge of the hurricane fence that surrounded a dog pen. It was tall, with barbed wire across the top. As the dogs hurled their bodies against the fence it clanged, the sound punctuating their howling like an anvil playing counterpoint to the hounds of hell.

"And what there is, we'll drag out. Bury somewhere"—he gestured—"out there in the woods. Or maybe we'll throw it in a croker sack and take a drive over to Lake Lanier. Couple of big rocks, and that sack'll disappear in the deep water. That's what happens to ladies what poke their noses in where they don't belong. Even pretty ladies."

"People know I've been here," Sam said. "I left word. They'll come looking for me. Looking for you, Buford."

"I like that," he said, pausing for a moment and then jerking her around to face him. "You never called me by my first name before. I like the way you say it. Say it again."

She was silent.

Once again he leaned down and forced his tongue into her mouth.

"You son-of-a-bitch," she spat when he released her.

He laughed. "I like 'em feisty, too."

Then he pushed her to her knees.

"You know about pit bulls?" he asked.

She twisted sideways, but he was ready for her. He still had a hand on her neck. Then he was on his knees, holding on. She kicked, but it was like kicking a wall. He loomed above her, straddling her as she twisted beneath him, her arms locked beneath her back. Her head was within inches of the fence now. The dogs were slavering on the other side, screaming in her ears. She could feel their wet breaths. They were dying for the taste of her.

"They're fighting bulls," Dodd told her. "I train them on a treadmill to be tough. Lock them by the collar to the treadmill and make them work till they're foaming at the mouth, till they puke. Builds muscles and guts.

"We have fights for money about once a month. Once a bull clamps on, he don't let loose. Not even when the blood stops spurting. They can't hear you anymore once they taste the blood. They just hold on. You have to hit 'em sometimes to get 'em to let go even when the other dog's dead, hit 'em with a crowbar.

"If they do let go before that, if they turn chicken, lose heart, I shoot 'em. Or kick 'em to death. No point in feeding a dog like that. Sets a bad example for the others, if you know what I mean.

"Hee-ah, boys!" he called again. The dogs screamed back. The sound of Dodd's voice was driving them into a frenzy.

Throughout this monologue, Sam hadn't stopped struggling.

He lowered his face until it was almost touching hers. "It makes me hot when you move like that." He reached down and jerked up her skirt. "Now, this part isn't going to hurt."

"This part is," said a voice from the darkness.

Dodd sat up abruptly. His mouth fell open. He jerked Sam to him with one hand and reached for his revolver with the other.

"Don't even think about it!" the voice said. "Hands up!"

Dodd wavered.

"Up!" the young woman commanded.

It was Totsie's voice! Totsie Kay was standing there, arms forward like a wedge, legs apart.

She stepped closer. "I'm very impatient. And my mama trained me to be a hell of a shot. Let Sam go. *Now.*" Her voice jumped on the last word.

Dodd was still hedging his bets. He held on.

Totsie adjusted her aim by a hair and fired. Just to the right and behind them in the darkness, a dog screamed, then gargled blood.

"You bitch!" Dodd roared. "Bastard! You killed my dog!"

"I'll kill you too if you don't let her go. *Move!*"

What a piece of work you are, Totsie Kay, Sam thought. What a gutsy piece of work.

Dodd tried another weapon, his tongue. "You killed

your boyfriend, bitch. No matter what happens here, you'll fry for that!"

"No, you didn't, Totsie!" Sam cried. "Don't listen to him. You didn't kill Ridley. *He* did!"

"Shut up!" Dodd growled.

"I know," Totsie said softly, speaking to Sam. "I know." She managed a wry grin. "When I pulled my gun out of the glove compartment tonight, I realized it was fully loaded. It hadn't been fired. I never shot it at the falls."

"*You* killed him!" Dodd insisted.

Totsie's voice rose again. "*You* shut up! I told you to let her go!"

Dodd held on.

"You bastard! This is your last warning. I'm counting to two. *One.*"

Still he didn't loosen his hold.

"*Two.*"

Totsie's gun jumped twice.

Buford Dodd screamed and slid to the ground, where he moaned and twitched, but he didn't rise.

"Totsie!" Sam scrambled up awkwardly and ran toward the girl, who was still holding the gun in both hands, frozen in a firing stance.

Totsie dropped the gun and threw her arms around Sam.

"Oh, my God! You saved me!" Sam cried.

"You saved *me!*"

Buford Dodd, shot neatly through both knees, mewled and twisted in the dirt. "Help me! Help me!" he pleaded.

Totsie turned. "I ought to kill you," she spat. Then she reached down and picked up her pistol.

"No, Totsie!" Sam cried.

"Oh, I'm not going to waste the lead," Totsie replied, leaning over Dodd. "I just want to make sure he holds still while I find the key to those cuffs."

Sam hadn't realized that her wrists were still locked.

Totsie turned Dodd's hips and found what she was looking for on his belt.

"I'm dying!" he groaned.

"No, you're not," said Totsie. "I wouldn't think of letting you do that. I want you to live for a long, long time. Crippled, crawling like a baby. Begging for somebody to help you up. Asking nicely. You're going to learn to say *pretty please,* Mr. Dodd."

Eighteen

◆

THERE WAS ALMOST NOTHING THAT PEACHES LIKED better than a party. She'd been humming around her kitchen for two days, plotting and planning, sautéeing and simmering.

Now the dining room table was laid with the white cutwork linen luncheon cloth, the gold-rimmed Spode, and the pistol-handled English silver. Miriam Talbot, who was to be one of the luncheon guests, had sent over a huge bouquet of her old-fashioned pink, cream, and yellow roses, which Peaches had arranged in a fat crystal vase on the sideboard.

"I'm in here, dear," George called when Samantha tapped on his door. "Come and get me."

"My, my," he said when she drew close enough for him to smell her perfume. "Aren't you a vision in yellow? It's perfect with your hair. You look not a day over nineteen."

Well, *that* was an exaggeration. But she knew she looked good. She'd set out to do so. After all, this was a celebration. She hadn't realized until she was already downstairs that the dress she was wearing was very similar to one she'd worn when she was just a girl—or had she?

She smiled at George. "And you're looking pretty gorgeous yourself."

He did cut a handsome figure in his beautifully tailored white spring jacket with the gold buttons bearing the crest of Yale, his alma mater, and his navy slacks. A trace of pink in his tie was just the touch to set off the color in his cheeks.

"Too bad you're not going to have a lady friend here today to see how spiffy you look," she said.

"How do you know I'm not?"

Sam stopped for a moment and ran down the guest list. "There's you, and me, and . . ." She paused. "Miriam. Miriam Talbot! Are you teasing me?"

"A gentleman never teases in affairs of the heart," he said, smiling.

"Why, *George!*"

"Why, what?"

Then Horace announced the lady in question on the intercom, and they went out to greet her.

Miriam was beautiful in a baby-blue dress of old-fashioned dotted swiss, which was perfect with her eyes and snowy hair. She smiled as George kissed her on the cheek.

"My dear," she murmured.

Beau was right behind Miriam. Well, he'd worked on the case. Sam had *had* to invite him. His silver hair was still damp from his shower. Sam narrowed her eyes as he beamed at her. He was too handsome to be up to any good in a gray and white seersucker suit and a red bow tie.

"All you need is a boater," she said with a laugh.

With a flourish, he produced from behind his back a straw hat of that very description, wrapped with a navy and red band. "Thought maybe I'd try to convince you to go for a spin in a canoe later."

That's what they'd done on their first date, gone for a canoe ride. She shot him a warning look.

"I love your dress. Awfully pretty." Then he grinned that grin, and she knew that he hadn't forgotten the yellow sundress either.

"Let's sit out on the porch and have a drink while we wait for Liza," George suggested. "I want to show off my new wicker furniture, and it's such a pretty day."

"A perfect day," Beau said to Sam, taking her arm as they strolled out to the porch, "for some storytelling. Now, I want to hear *all* the details, from the very beginning."

"Now, Beau," his mother chided, "maybe Samantha doesn't want to talk about all that at lunch."

"Mother, there is nothing that Sam Adams likes better than telling a good story."

"Yes, there is," her uncle disagreed. "Writing one."

"And that was a doozie that appeared on this morning's front page." Beau tipped the hat, which he was still holding, toward her. "Was Hoke pleased?"

"Yes." She grinned. "In a begrudging kind of way."

"Gin and tonic, please," Beau said in answer to Horace's silent query. "So, you got your corrupt sheriff and the answer to the Ridley mystery all rolled up into one. Couldn't have asked for it neater, Sam. But come on, give us the straight skinny, the stuff you didn't write for the paper."

"Well . . ." Sam settled into her chair and looked around at her audience. "I'll tell you the part about

213

Forrest Ridley before Liza gets here. There's no need for her to know all of this."

They nodded.

"Kay Kay *did* send the invitations to the party at the Ridleys. She got the idea from a story that Forrest had told about a practical joke he played when he was a law student."

"Her prints were on the follow-up note," Beau confirmed. "It was easy, once Sam told us who we were looking for."

"But why?" Miriam asked. "Why would a grown woman do a thing like that?"

"Because she knew her daughter was having an affair with Forrest Ridley. That was part of it. She wanted to shake him up. But mostly, I think, she did it because she hated Queen."

Miriam asked her next question with raised eyebrows.

"Queen was having an affair with her husband, Edison."

"My word!" Miriam cried. "That's all so sordid."

"Mom's led a very sheltered life." Beau patted her on the shoulder.

"As well she should. And we'll keep it that way." George smiled at Miriam, and then down at the magnificent new string of pearls she was wearing. He still had an excellent eye, for a man who was going blind. His latest gift looked beautiful on her.

"I don't think that affair between Queen and Edison had been going on awfully long, but long enough for Kay Kay to get wind of it," Sam continued. "And Queen knew about her husband and Totsie, which hurt her pride more than anything else—which was one reason she got involved with Edison. But when

Liza started asking questions about his being away—
at which point he was actually already dead—Queen
just wanted to put a lid on it. She figured he was with
Totsie somewhere, and his absence gave her a chance
to spend more time with Edison. Of course, Edison
really wasn't such a catch. I think that money, not
women, was his game, just as Kay Kay said. But for
Queen, besides revenge, there was the appeal of all
that money. Don't think she didn't notice that Edison
was doing *awfully* well."

"You mean you don't think she loved him," Miriam said.

"I'm not sure I think Queen Ridley ever loved
anyone except herself," Sam replied. "But she sure
picked wrong with Edison. What with the accessory-
to-murder charges, not to mention the drugs and the
land deals, it's going to be a very long time before
Edison Kay is a free man again."

"I never did like that man anyway," Miriam
sniffed.

"Me either," said Peaches, who had come in with a
plate of roasted pecans and cheese straws.

"I didn't know you knew him," Sam said, surprised.

"I know what I know," Peaches sniffed.

"I should have just asked her who the murderer was
in the first place," Sam said to George after Peaches
had left the porch.

"I always do," her uncle agreed.

"Well, why didn't you ask her this time?"

"I didn't want to mess in your business."

"Go 'way." She slapped at him.

"Don't you think Liza knows all this?" Beau asked.
"About Queen and her father and Totsie?"

"I think she suspects. And if she wants to know the details, she'll ask. I think she's protecting herself right now until she's through grieving for her father."

"I think you're right, dear," Miriam agreed.

The doorbell rang just then, and moments later Horace announced Liza. Sam stood to greet her, as did the two men, but when the young woman appeared on the porch, Sam stepped back a pace. She almost didn't recognize this new Liza, who had discarded her punk artist all-black costume and was now dressed head-to-toe in white. She was lovely.

"I'm nothing if not a creature of extremes," she said, laughing at Sam.

"And a very pretty one." Beau bent to kiss her on the cheek.

After a few moments of small talk, Liza turned to Sam. "I'm dying to hear about your grand escape."

Sam barely had her mouth open when Horace reappeared. "Lunch," he announced.

The meal began with vichyssoise and progressed to shrimp and lobster salad with Louis dressing.

"Now, Sam, I want to hear it," said Liza.

Sam took a deep breath to begin, but Peaches interrupted her. "I hope you're not going to talk about unpleasant things at my table and upset your digestion and ruin a good meal."

"Then you and Horace will join us afterwards for dessert, and I'll tell the rest of the story," Sam said.

"What about digesting dessert?" Beau whispered. Sam kicked him under the table.

"Sure, we can wait," said Liza. She hesitated, inspecting a beautiful piece of lobster. "After graduation next month, I'm going to live with my Aunt Jean in New York and study painting. She has a great loft in Soho."

"That's wonderful!" said Sam.

"I know." Liza's eyes were happy and shiny. No one asked what her mother was going to do alone, but Liza ventured a theory anyway. "Maybe Queen will go and live with Dr. Tuckit in Rio."

"Now," Peaches said to Sam as they all settled around the table in the screened gazebo where she had decreed that they should enjoy dessert, "shoot."

"So that night at the Kays', Totsie walked straight up the front stairs at her parents' house, and then right down the back stairs. And—"

Suddenly there was the thud of heavy footsteps on the brick driveway that curved around the side of the house, and a startling figure appeared.

"Good Lord, have mercy," Peaches cried. "Who . . . what . . . is that?"

Sam recognized the figure. "It's Herman Blanding." She rose. "Oh, my! Would you look?"

Mr. Blanding was a sight to behold in his full Civil War regalia. It was not the uniform he had worn when Sam called on him at home, but a dress suit complete with a sword in a shining scabbard. He was rather elegant. His hair was even combed. And instead of his usual pallor, the color was high in his face.

"I've come to slay the man who killed Forrest Ridley," he announced, brandishing his sword as he approached the door of the gazebo.

"Lord and the saints preserve us," Peaches whispered.

Horace stepped out and took Mr. Blanding by the arm.

"Sorry." Blanding tipped his hat. The plume brushed the grass. "I knocked for a long time on the front door. I didn't mean to barge in like this."

"Mr. Blanding," Horace said as if this were an everyday occurrence, "won't you come and join us for some dessert?"

"Have you lost your mind?" Peaches hissed.

"I can't. I have to kill the man." Blanding stood at attention. "It came to me in a dream."

"Are you sure you won't join us?" Samantha called. "We have homemade raspberry sorbet and Peaches' famous coconut cake."

"No." Blanding's jaw was strong, as was his resolve. "I must stand guard."

"I'm sure he'll be perfectly all right," Miriam said to Peaches in a low voice. Miriam Talbot had seen more than a few Southern eccentrics in her sixty-odd years and considered herself a good judge of them. "Just leave him be for a while. He'll simmer down. Now, go on with your story, Samantha."

"As I was saying . . ." Sam leaned into her chair and continued for the fourth time. "Totsie skipped down the back stairs. She figured she was in so much trouble . . ." Sam looked at Liza, who waved her on. Either Liza knew or she didn't want to know, but in any case, Sam didn't have to explain that part. ". . . in so much trouble that she'd get out of there and go to her apartment and sleep in her own bed. But what she saw when she stepped outside was Buford Dodd pulling out behind my car with no lights on."

"So she followed," said Beau.

"Yes. We must have made quite a parade. Me, toodling along, too fast probably, but never thinking to look back. Dodd behind me in his dark patrol car.

And then Totsie behind him, also with no lights. It's a wonder somebody didn't come along and crash into us.

"When Totsie saw Dodd pull me from my car, she knew she'd done the right thing. So she just kept on following."

"Still with no lights?" George asked.

"Partly. Once we got on I-75, she knew she was okay. She doused them again, of course, when Dodd pulled down the little dirt lane toward the dogs." Sam shuddered involuntarily.

"Oh, my dear!" Miriam said. "That must have been so awful."

"It was. I thought I was dead."

"You would have been," said Liza, "if Totsie hadn't saved you. I'll always have to be grateful to her for that."

And then Sam knew that Liza knew the whole story about Totsie and her dad, but had come to terms with it.

"Did you have an escape plan?" Beau asked.

"I wish I could say yes, but I'm afraid I would have been a goner if Totsie hadn't come after me," Sam admitted. "She *is* a crack shot. Kay Kay did one whale of a job training her."

"I'll kill him," Mr. Blanding started up again out in the yard.

"Now, Mr. Blanding, sir," Horace called. "You're going to have to quiet down."

Beau leaned toward Sam's ear. "I'd have died if anything had happened to you. Won't you come with me after lunch? I need to talk with you."

She felt herself softening a little. She never should have worn this damned yellow dress.

"Going to call him out and challenge him to a duel!" Blanding shouted.

"You don't need to do that." Samantha stood, stepped through the gazebo door into the soft grass, and took Blanding's hand. "The villain's been taken care of, Herman. Somebody else drilled him. It's okay."

"Oh." Herman Blanding blinked, and then blinked again. "Oh. All right. In that case"—and he stepped forward smiling that lovely sweet smile that Sam remembered from the day he'd served her tea and animal crackers and reminisced about his Susan—"in that case, I believe I *will* have a piece of that coconut cake."

SARAH SHANKMAN

SHE WALKS IN BEAUTY

A SAMANTHA ADAMS NOVEL

COMING SOON IN HARDCOVER
FROM POCKET BOOKS

POCKET
BOOKS